FARZANEH

AND THE

MOON

MATT WILVEN

Legend Press Ltd, 107-111 Fleet Street, London, EC4A 2AB
info@legend-paperbooks.co.uk | www.legendpress.co.uk

Contents © Matt Wilven 2019
The right of the above author to be identified as the author of this work has
been asserted in accordance with the Copyright, Designs and Patents Act
1988. British Library Cataloguing in Publication Data available.

Print ISBN 978-1-78955-0-245
Ebook ISBN 978-1-78955-0-238
Set in Times. Printing managed by Jellyfish Solutions Ltd
Cover design by Steve Marking | www.stevemarking.com

Matt Wilven was born in Blackpool in 1982. After receiving an MA with Distinction in Creative Writing, he spent the next ten years moving around, working jobs and honing his craft. His debut novel, *The Blackbird Singularity*, was published by Legend Press in 2016 and he was named as one of WHSmith's Fresh Talents in 2017. He lives and writes in London.

Visit Matt at
www.mattwilven.com
or on Twitter
@mattwilven

For Paul

"The moon is no door."

– Sylvia Plath

PART ONE

PART ONE

ONE

I'm leaning on the backdoor frame watching Farzaneh dig a hole in the centre of the lawn. The conifers along the fence are creaking while the smell of autumn decay drifts in around me. She has been fasting for two weeks, but her movements are effective and full of vigour.

"Nearly full moon," she says, finally noticing me, a white light of excitement in her eyes.

"I didn't realise it was today."

"Fourteen days, eighteen hours," she replies, striking the shovel back into the ground with a grin. "You knew it was today."

Farzaneh walks around the hole to check that all the angles are sharp enough. After kneeling down and chiselling at one of the corners, she stands up, takes a step back and raises her chest. I approach the hole and look down. It's about two feet deep. The corners are perfect right angles.

As arranged, Farzaneh puts the snorkel mask on, steps into the hole and lies down. She has bent the air pipe so that it points upwards. It rises just above ground level. I look up into the dark morning for a second, then grab the shovel, scoop up a mound of earth and scatter it over her legs. She pulls the pipe from her mouth and the mask from her face.

"Wait," she says, standing up, patting the mud from her trousers. "I was just checking. I have to be naked."

She takes off her top, folds it up, places it by the side of the hole and then does the same with her trousers and underwear. Her legs are thin, almost straight along the bone. Her pelvis looks as though it might puncture her skin. She straightens her spine and looks up at some parting black clouds, her ribs raked and stark.

"Okay," she says. "It's time."

She puts the snorkel mask back on and lies down in the hole again. I start by covering her feet, gently scattering the earth in case there are any stones in it.

"Six thirteen," she says, pulling the pipe from her mouth. "I need to be underground for six thirteen."

I nod and shovel quicker, filling the side of the hole where her legs are, up to her pelvis and then over the indented space that used to be her stomach. As I fling the mud and dirt, Farzaneh is collected and still, centred and in position. Her body is taut. Her eyes, behind the plastic of the snorkel mask, are focused on the sky above.

I turn my head and check the clock on the wall in the kitchen. Five past six. I carry on, heaving mud over her sunken chest and scrawny neck. As I get to her head it's hard to remain calm about the fact that this is happening, that this is what she wants. I tell myself that the burial is going to remove her desire to reach out into the beyond, that when I dig her up she'll really be here, back in this world. I kneel down and look into her eyes.

"Are you sure it has to be an hour?" I ask. "It seems too long."

Her eyes move up, to the side and then right back at me. She is contemptuously telling me to carry on, suggesting that the timing of all this is crucial and that the hour is non-negotiable. I take one last look at her face and begin to cover her head. She's underground for just after ten past six.

Once she's buried and I'm alone in the garden something comes undone inside me. I imagine myself performing a manic, celebratory death dance around the filled-in hole. This is followed by an urge to smash the shovel down to the earth where her face and lungs are. I want to jump all over her, stamp on her and pour dirt down the snorkel pipe so that she really does disappear into the mud. Instead, I gently level out the ground with the tip of the shovel, equating a flatter surface with a more balanced outcome, and then sit cross-legged, occasionally lowering my ear to the inch of black snorkel pipe popping up, trying but failing to hear her breathe.

The full moon begins to pass through a break in the clouds, pristine and bright. It's in the portion of the sky that Farzaneh looked at before she lay down to be buried, about to reach the instant of its totality. I sense its fullness, the sheer clarity of its form, but also the consummation between her and it, the loss of her to it. There is a whisper in the white light around me, the vague suggestion of a place beyond what is shown.

As dawn approaches, the gleam of the full moon begins to dampen and the white edges of the broken clouds turn to bronze. The sky loses the depth of its blackness and begins to haze into dark blue. My thighs jig up and down. I want to know what's going on underground. Does she find the blackness soothing? Is the weight of the soil crushing her? Is it cold or warm? Are there creatures slithering around her? Crawling on her? Into her?

I twist my neck and check the clock in the kitchen. It's still before seven. There's over fifteen minutes left but I can't wait any longer. With a spasmodic lurch, I claw at the cold ground where her head and shoulders are, digging with my hands so that I don't hurt her with the shovel, frenetic but also careful not to knock any dirt into the pipe. I'm imagining limbs turning black, fingers and toes falling off, a gasp for air that has filled her mouth with mud. I want her to have the experience she needs but I don't want any harm to come to her. From what she has told me, neither does she.

When I can see the shadowy outline of the snorkel mask in the hole I have to take a moment to calm myself. I carefully wipe the plastic of the eye-piece clear with the back of my index finger. Her eyes are open, flicking this way and that as though she's halfway between awake and dreaming. I pause, unsure of how to proceed, but a cloud shifts, revealing the moon that had been briefly cloaked. Its light penetrates her pupils and strikes her retinas. They stop flitting about, her spine jerks and she sits up with a sharp, silent motion. Dark earth falls away from her hair and shoulders and her body begins to shake. I grab her jumper and wrap it around her. The skin on her back looks bruised – not her usual tea colour – but I can't see anything properly because of the twilight. She looks dark blue, green, purple; a different colour every second.

I dig mud away from around her pelvis while she fails to take the snorkel mask from her face three times. She starts gasping from around the mouth piece, gulping at the air as though her body has just remembered that it needs to breathe, looking at me through the mask as if to ask what I'm doing, who am I, what is this world? I pull the pipe from her mouth. With the flow of air to her lungs unimpeded, the pieces start coming back together. She pulls off the mask and looks straight ahead, regulating her breath with a look of disdain, as though respiration is a weakness that she had temporarily risen above.

Scooping the mud out from around her legs, the pitch of the light in the garden shifts and I feel the inclination to turn around. I look up at the first-floor window and see that the old woman from the flat upstairs is staring down from a light-filled triangle, pinching her curtain, grimacing and trying to decipher the confusing shadowy images in the garden. I turn back to Farzaneh and pull at the cold mud where her legs are, ignoring our voyeur. Getting her out of the ground is more important.

When I get down to her feet they are dark and slightly swollen. I look back up at the old woman's window. She's still there. I wave my arms around at her, agitated. She still doesn't move. I walk towards the house for a second and make the same gestures. The light from the kitchen must hit my body

14

at this point because she snaps into herself and disappears behind her curtains. I go back to Farzaneh who is juddering in the hole. Things are crawling on her. Maybe it's just my eyes.

"Come on. Let's get you inside," I say, pulling her up. "I'll run you a bath."

Dirt falls from between her narrow legs. She is muddy, distant, shaking with dark knowledge. I guide her into the house with my shoulder beneath her armpit. She knocks her hip on the kitchen table, then on the fridge. In the doorway to the bathroom she stops, unsure of how to proceed. I lean her against the doorframe and start running a bath.

As the tub fills I wrap her in towels and start scouring at the mud on her body. I realise that I can only smear it around, and that the towel is getting filthy, so I focus more on creating friction to warm her. Once the bath is full I lead her to its side, holding her waist and wrist, but I can't find the words that will get her to climb in. She just stares down at it. I have to pick her up and lower her into the water. I'm worried about the temperature and ask her if it's too hot but she doesn't respond.

Ultraviolet pinks and purples gleam in through the frosted glass of the bathroom window. The sun is beginning to rise. I rub soap into her neck and shoulders. Her goose-bumps thicken as she passes from frozen to cold. My hand snags on her hair while I'm scrubbing mud from her neck and a clump pulls out, leaving a thinned, bald patch behind her ear. The pain sparks a flash of consciousness in her eyes.

"Clss-sss-sss," she says, her teeth chattering, bath mist rising around her.

"What's that, Far? What did you say?"

"Clss... ss, ss, clse," she says, a faint smile appearing and disappearing as the light fades from her eyes.

I decide against shampooing her hair and rinse it gently instead. Each time I raise the plastic jug the bath water is darker. I'm hoping that she's going to reveal something about her time underground but she's silent. Her eyes look into an invisible distance. She hasn't come back.

TWO

I arrive in London with a backpack full of weed, a scratched-up skateboard and a worn copy of *The Last Days of Socrates*. The rest of my stuff is being sent down in a van. Finding the right Underground line is simple but satisfactory. A sign that I'm going to survive. The Tube air tastes stagnant and the passengers are all dead-eyed or gazing down at phone screens as the carriage rattles and sways. Mile End seems familiar enough: terraces, council blocks, families, students, tough-looking kids. No one bats an eyelid at the noise of my skateboard coming up behind them. The city has dulled their nerves.

I go to the campus office, sign a couple of things and pick up my keys. It turns out my room is in an old morgue. Across the way there's a much bigger building that used to be a hospital. There are squeals of excitement and trills of laughter coming from that building. The morgue is quiet. Maybe I got lucky, maybe I didn't.

Down my corridor there are twelve bedrooms, four toilets, four showers and two small kitchens. The walls are all institutional beige. In my room there's a single bed, a half-size wardrobe, a bookshelf, a small sink and mirror, and a desk. The paint is chipped where posters have been pulled off the walls. There's a laminated A4 printout on the bare mattress with ten rules and the first one, written in bold print, is: *DO NOT PUT*

POSTERS ON THE WALLS. I smile. My window looks out onto a strip of weeping willows that hang down by a canal. Things could be worse.

My stuff arrives and the man in the van doesn't get a tip because he stands around idly while I schlep to and fro with my boxes. The first thing I do is set up my laptop and speakers, put some music on and smoke a joint out of my window. I try to imagine my future in London, my new friends, the things I'll learn on my course, but it's impossible.

Once I finish the joint, I sit on the bare mattress staring into space until an excitable girl with lots of bangles on her wrists knocks on my door and invites me to a fresher's party over at the old hospital. It's nothing special. She goes down the whole corridor inviting everybody.

At the party a large sound system pumps out old pop songs with dance beats forged over them. The biggest room is a communal space up on the second floor with vending machines and a pool table. I take one of my cans of lager out of my backpack and lean against a wall. Out of one of the windows, I can see the tips of the brightly lit skyscrapers in Canary Wharf popping up over a dark mass of buildings. I'm in London, I realise.

There must be close to two hundred people milling in and out of the room. Groups are forming in random, unbound clusters; eyes full of fear, laughter coming too easily, everybody's teeth showing. I see two chatty, preppy-looking guys break away from one gathering, glad to have found each other, egos boosted by the fact that they are leaving six others floundering in a silent, friendless chaos.

A bunch of the more confident suburban kids are trying out their bedroom dance moves on a makeshift dancefloor. There's a skinny lad with an expensive haircut sitting outside the entrance to the toilets with his drunken mind spinning between his knees. A plump girl is sitting on her haunches, trying to comfort him, masking her loneliness in his suffering. A small mass of black clothing in one corner is having a particularly powerful gravitational effect on the other items of black clothing scattered around the room. I can't tell if they're goths or fashion victims, or both. Right in front of me, an Asian girl in a purple-and-white cosplay outfit trips and falls to the floor and starts laughing hysterically. She won't let her friend pick her up. She's revelling in it.

I smell pot in the air so I light one of the joints I rolled up in my room. Once it's clear that I'm smoking weed a blonde girl in a shiny black top comes over to me. She asks what course I'm doing, where I'm from and what music I'm into: "Philosophy." "Manchester." "All sorts." She's hot but she's not listening. She's not even looking at me. She just wants me to pass her the joint. When she senses that it's not coming her way she glances back over at her group of equally hot, just-laid-eyes-on-each-other-but-friends-for-life girlfriends.

"So, me and my friends were wondering if we could steal a joint off you."

"I only brought enough for me."

"But it's weed. You have to share weed. It's, like, the rules."

She follows this statement with a look that says, You want to fuck me so you'll give me whatever I want. Her posture and facial expressions come from the internet, not real life. I imagine too many teenage masturbators have liked her posts and pictures. Their lust has made her stupid.

"A spliff," I say, attempting to channel Socrates, "isn't shared because it gets shared, it gets shared because it's being shared."

She frowns at me with a half-grimace, trying to let me know that intelligence is ugly.

"How about you just share the rest of that?"

"Sure. Stick around. You can bum twos."

She's disgusted by the idea of staying and talking to me, and the word 'bum' has exposed her misguided sense of entitlement and the fact that, in essence, she's begging. Her face contorts. She almost laughs but shakes her head instead.

She turns away from me and walks back over to her friends swinging her hips and shrugging.

Before I can blink a sandy-skinned rich boy with a pounding, overconfident voice is trying his luck. He's been in Africa all summer, owns a kayak. My disinterest in his travelling seems to be worrying him on a deep but visible level. He's flicking his diagonal blonde fringe back again and again in a way that looks like a nervous tick. To get things on track, to get closer to procuring the joint, he asks what course I'm doing, where I'm from and what music I'm into: "Philosophy." "Manchester." "All sorts." He looks at the joint every time I answer. He does it so blatantly that I move it here and there just to watch his head bob about. When he finally notices that I'm making a fool of him he laughs at the transparency of his self-interest and taps me on the shoulder.

"Worth a try, eh?"

"Was it?" I ask.

Before he leaves his face straightens. He looks down at the joint for a moment, thinks about asking for it anyway, looks up into my eyes, decides against it and then goes on his way.

The girl who comes over next has no neck and walks like a stout middle-aged man. Her hair is all over the place in a manner contrived to make her look rushed, and too interesting to be vain, but it comes off as desperate and neurotic. When she asks me what course I'm doing I sigh and tell her that if she wants some of my joint she should just come out and ask for it.

"Life," she says, "is too short to stand around talking to wankers. Even if they do have weed."

She turns and waddles away.

I smile, suddenly liking her. I almost follow her to make amends but I can't muster the effort. I'm not sure I'm in the right mood for this party. I finish my can and my joint, coming round to the idea of going back to my room, but when I take my weight off the wall a moment of optimism urges me to stay. I don't want to give up on my first night in London so easily. I told myself I'd try to be less critical when I got here, more open to things. I lean back against the wall and take another beer out of my backpack.

Nobody approaches me until I light my second joint. Straight away a lanky ginger lad in a pale blue Manchester City football shirt marches towards me. The closer he gets, the faster he gets. He tramps right into me. He's about six foot four so his bony chest hits my face. I push him away. He steps back and looks into my eyes, a churlish grin cutting into his cheeks. He raises a joint to his mouth, my joint, and takes a long, deep drag. I check my hand. It's really gone.

"Hey," I say, reaching out to get it back.

"One second," he replies, holding out his long thin arm to keep me at bay, a bony forefinger poised in front of my nose.

He takes another two quick, sharp blasts and inhales them as one. Blood rushes into his brain and his hand wavers into my cheek. I deflect it away with a snap of my wrist and go for the joint again.

"You're toenailing it," I say.

He arches his back away from me, to keep the joint out of reach, and steals another drag. I lean back against the wall, feigning detachment and disinterest, but this only invigorates him to inhale an extra flurry of tiny toots. His guiltless opportunism is almost as impressive as it is annoying. I smile in disbelief.

As satisfaction eases its way into the lines of his face, he exhales a giant plume of smoke, slouches onto the wall next to me and offers up the joint. It's squashed and half smoked down one side. I take it and start trying to fix the toenail with my lighter.

"I needed that," he says.

"You wrecked it."

"I treated it right."

"You just came up and taxed me."

"You were monopolising an unregulated market. I had to step in. It was a matter of social justice."

I eye him, curious. He stretches out his drunken arms above his head and gestures the party.

"Look at these fuckers."

"What about them?" I say, still sorting out the toenail.

"*Look* at them."

I want to dislike him but I can't. I'm smiling.

"You're from Manchester?" I ask.

He puts his left fist on his chest, his right fist up into the air and begins singing, his face up to the ceiling:

"*Blue moon, you saw me standing alone, without a dream in my heart, without a love of my own.*"

"Me too," I say, taking a couple of drags and then passing the joint back his way.

He takes it, smirking. He likes that I'm ignoring his bullshit.

"Pretty bold, smoking weed in public on the first night. You must want people to know what a massive rebel you are."

"I just smoke weed. That's all."

"Gotcha. Downbeat. Cool. That's your thing."

"I don't have a thing."

"Touchy, aren't you?" he says. He begins a deadpan impression of me. "Don't put me in a box. I'm undefinable. I'm unique." He goes back to being himself. "I'm going to call you Baby. Nobody puts Baby in a corner."

"What?"

"Relax, Baby. Relax."

He passes the joint back. I take a drag.

"Baby?" I ask.

He doesn't hear me.

"Look at these fuckers," he says, again.

"I'm looking."

"This town is going to tear them to shreds."

"What makes you think that?"

"Look," he says, taking the joint and pointing across the room. "There's a phone on that table, a bag under that chair, and that one. Two phones on that table. They're idiots. I'm

21

Jake by the way. I'm studying economics and I don't care what kind of music you're into."

I smile and take the joint back.

"Maybe they'd be more careful if they were out and about. They live here. Everybody's in the same boat."

"Trust no one," says Jake.

"No. I know. But…"

"Trust no one," he repeats.

"But now, if I trust no one, I'm trusting you."

"That's a very good point. Let me guess, you're studying… law?"

"Philosophy."

"This might work," he says. "We'll give it a go. You've got more pot, right?"

"At least you're honest."

"Sweet fucking Jesus," he says, looking at a girl's cleavage as she passes. "I wish I had half a clue why so many of these girls are dressed like Bladerunner robo-whores. Maybe I'll ask her."

He dashes off after the girl with the cleavage. She has big eyes, big breasts and a tiny waist and she's far too attractive for him. I see her folding her arms and eyeing his football shirt with contempt but he's still cocksure and chipper when he comes back over.

"I'm none the wiser," he says. "I mean, look at her. She's basically in fancy dress."

"She got your attention."

"Of course she did. She may as well have a neon sign above her head saying *tits*."

"Women must love you."

"I'm a lamb beneath it all," he says, watching another girl go by, narrowing his eyes and pursing his lips.

Jake goes on three more failed missions to talk to girls. I stand around and wait for him to come back and tell me about them. His observations are funny and cringe-worthy in equal measure. My intuition is telling me that I like him so I just ignore half of what he says and trust my gut.

We leave around three in the morning and swap numbers. Walking back across to the morgue I don't feel as alone as I did before the party. There are millions of people sprawled across this city and I know one of them. There's a new name in my phone. Things are going to be okay.

THREE

Jake leads the way, down a side corridor in the old hospital, barging past people queuing anxiously outside a bedroom. I follow with my head down, trying to ignore their glares. He's taking me to buy weed. I don't need weed. I've got over half an ounce stashed away in my room. I just pretended I didn't have any because he's been smoking mine non-stop for two weeks.

In the room, Shaun, a pot dealer with a steroid problem, is putting tiny buds on a digital scale at his desk. His muscles are abnormally large and his eyes are analysing the little nubs of cannabis with an electrical tinge of craziness. Jake pre-emptively told me that Shaun is re-sitting his first year in Film Studies for the third time, laughing about what a 'pleb' he is.

The room is full. There's an in-crowd sitting around on the bed and floor and a line of students waiting to be served. Jake walks past them, puts his hand on Shaun's shoulder and starts his queue-jumping schmooze. I loiter by the doorway, my eyes wandering over faces until I begin to fixate on a girl sitting in the centre of the bed.

Her eyes are wide and black and she's inside herself in a way I've never seen before. She's continually expressing a flux of thoughts and emotions: agreement, empathy, understanding… dismissal, irony, amusement… fear, antagonism, outrage. Yet, the thing that keeps me looking isn't the dramatic fluidity of her reactions but the intensity of them. Her eyes are vacuums, too eager and too hungry, and they have an inverse effect; making everybody else eager and hungry for her. A deep and primal portion of my brain is telling me that part of my future was arranged before I got here, that it has to be her, it was always going to be her.

I stare for so long that she senses my gaze and glances over. Her look lingers longer than most would dare or bother. There's no fear in her. She sees that I'm transfixed and the corner of her mouth curls up. My stomach flips and I flick my eyes away. When I look back she's involved in the conversation again. Fully and completely engaged. I want to walk over, join the group, but somehow that space, just two metres away, seems as though it's at the other end of an impossible bridge. She lives in a world I can't access. I'll never get there.

A thin, slimy tongue licks my cheek.

"You'd love a piece of that wrapped around your cock," says Jake, whispering into my ear in a mock-erotic tone.

I wipe my wet cheek with my sleeve.

"Why do you act even more creepy than you actually are?"

"I thought a little lick might help you get rid of your boner."

I know I'm not erect but I still look down. Jake smirks and then waggles a tiny bag of weed so that it flicks against my nose.

"What's that?" I ask.

"Weed."

"Where's the rest of it? I gave you twenty."

"London, mate. London… Seriously though, I wouldn't let Shaun catch you gawping."

I hadn't even realised that I was looking at her again. I turn my body towards Jake.

"Why? What do you mean?"

"Farzaneh. She's his bird."

"She's with *him*?"

25

"Say it a bit louder. I don't think every member of his gym heard you."

"Seriously?" I whisper. "She seems more… I don't know."

Jake looks over at Shaun, pausing for effect.

"Size matters."

The next night I show up at Shaun's room on my own, daring myself to buy weed and sit down with the in-crowd – just so I can see Farzaneh – but the door is shut and there's no one around. I knock anyway. Shaun answers, gloomy, the sour fug of skunk weed all around him.

"You got anything?" I ask.

He looks back into the room, sighs and nods his head. I follow him in. He gets a small, empty baggie off his desk and sits down on the bed, gathering up bits of weed from his own personal tray. The room is empty except for Farzaneh, sitting beside him with an open book she's not reading in her hands. She puts the book down, lazily hangs an arm over Shaun's neck and starts gently rubbing his bicep, watching him put the weed in the baggie. Her eyes are vacant. Her body is here, in this world, but she's somewhere else.

"Quiet tonight," I say.

Neither of them respond. Farzaneh's eyes don't even flicker. Shaun keeps his head down, pinching and plucking at bits of weed.

"Here," he says, closing the seal and holding it out without looking up.

I take it and pass him the money. He grabs the note and discards it onto the bed without checking to see if it's the right amount.

"Okay," I say. "Thanks."

I step back, daring, for a moment, to keep looking at Farzaneh. Even in this state of departure there's something about her. She's anchored to her centre. She behaves as she is, without filters or pretence. I imagine finding the right words or action to jolt her into life, seeing the eager energy of last night reappear in her body and eyes, but the way she's attached to Shaun, stroking him, it's clear that she's already where she wants to be. I nod, making a decision to move on, and leave them to it.

FOUR

My Philosophy course is a non-starter when it comes to making friends. A weirdly large proportion of the boys have grasshopper-shaped heads and dermatological issues: acne on the cheekbones, flaky scalps, waxy red hands, rash climbing the neck, blotchy red spots on the forearms, inflamed eyelids. The guy who seems the smartest, with the most on-point responses in class and no awkwardness about his gawky frame or his five dry knuckle warts, is also intolerably arrogant. The few girls scattered around the lecture halls all seem to crave invisibility, hiding their faces behind their hair and hands, wearing baggy fisherman's jumpers and thick-rimmed glasses. They slink into the most isolated chairs and disappear at the end of lectures before you can even look up. They are all, boys and girls alike, bookish and anxious, with highly developed critical faculties, and so either behave standoffishly or retreat into their shells when they are approached. Every day it seems like another one of them glances down at the skateboard I'm carrying and decides that I'm an idiot who chose the wrong course. No conversations are sparking up.

I'm reading Aristotle's *Ethics* in my room for my first assignment on meta-ethics, normative ethics and practical ethics. The lectures and seminars are interesting but I'm finding the book difficult. When Jake knocks on my door he easily talks me into a daytime pint in the Student's Union.

Sitting with our drinks, I confess that I can't get Farzaneh out of my head.

"She's definitely a two tissue tug," he says, "but, even if she wasn't shagging the incredible hulk, she's too complicated, and too clever, and too fucking hot. You need to have some fun, screw around a bit. There are hundreds of normals gagging for a trendy little skater-boy like you and you're walking around blind to it all."

"Trendy little skater-boy?"

He laughs at me. He laughs at anything other people take seriously about themselves and I find it to be one of his more grounding qualities.

"It's okay, Baby," he says. "I'm not trying to put you in a corner. But you must know what you look like."

I don't think of myself as looking a certain way. I usually just wear a plain black hoodie and dark blue jeans. It's an attempt to be invisible; a way of dressing that means chavs and thugs tend to leave me alone when I'm out on the streets skating. The idea that this is a style, and that girls are into it, is weird to me. When Jake peels his Manchester City football shirt off he tends to wear dark colours with bright trims; all mid-range designer, all smart-casual, all fashionable. I suppose lots of people think they're invisible in their own way.

"I guess I think of myself as nondescript," I say.

"Yeah, right. You're so normcore."

"Why are you obsessed with normalness all of a sudden?"

He ignores me and starts doing something peculiar with his eyebrows.

"Here, check out this blonde with the rack. If a cheeky look at those watermelons doesn't get Farzaneh out your system, I don't know what will "

I look over my shoulder and see her.

"We both know you wouldn't know what to do with watermelons. You wouldn't know what to do with tangerines."

"Oh, I'd know what to do," he assures me.

I shake my head and smile.

We end up drinking pints until the early evening. By the time girls are turning up in perfume and make-up we're drunk. Jake announces that we have to skip dinner and power through. He claims that the Student's Union is the ideal place to practice his 'dustpan-and-brush treatment' (this involves him picking up girls and gathering phone numbers in the very last minutes after the lights come up, 'when desperation sets in').

By nine o'clock Jake is over-eager and talking to everyone.

"Alright, lads!" he shouts to a group at the foosball table as we walk back from the bar. "Go on, son!" he yells at a couple kissing, mustering laughter from those around them.

He's a walking, talking cliché machine but, somehow, a glimmer of irony saves him from the severity of obnoxiousness. People love him.

"You're full of it tonight," I say.

"I'm the most valuable asset on the free market. Looky over here."

He grabs my arm and pulls me towards a bunch of girls. All blonde and all dressed in pastels, golds and bronzes.

"Well, hell-o, ladies," he says. The pack opens up, amused. "Look at the way they've lined up for us. It's like we're the corporate elite choosing high-class sex workers. Pankhurst must be spinning in her grave."

They release a gust of gasps and giggles.

"Now, ladies, you have to be gentle with my friend here. He's not like the rest of us. He's deeply sensitive, and exquisitely unique."

They all laugh. I look to the side and shake my head.

"What do you think?" he says, looking at me. "They don't look too scary, do they? None of you bite, do you?" He winks.

"I do," says one of them.

They laugh.

"Well, you better stay away from my friend here. I'm going to have to talk to you."

Jake starts in on the girl who claims she bites, asking what course she's doing, where she's from and what music she's into. The skinniest and most sympathetic looking of the group steps towards me and we end up having a stilted, non-hormone-induced conversation about avant-garde dance troupes (she studies Modern Dance). She's called Claire and she's got small beady eyes and a way of holding her mouth when she's listening that looks like she's either experiencing stomach cramps or struggling to understand simple language. She checks her phone, out of habit, not boredom, roughly every two and a half minutes.

I look at Jake with his bolshie blonde and wonder how he finds the enthusiasm to pretend he's so interested in her. Does having sex provide him with that much meaning? Or is it something else that turns his light on? He's not very good looking himself. His bony face is scarred from acne and he looks to have grown tall so quickly in his early teens that his back is a little bit bent. It's possible that he's insecure about his long, skeletal frame and makes up for it with a persona of confidence. Maybe he thinks he will never get to have sex unless he behaves this way. Or perhaps he just loves the thrill of the chase. Whatever his reasons, his approach trivialises sex, turns it into a game that he wants to win, and, since he's not handsome, I imagine that this is unattractive to most women.

I've got no idea what Claire has been talking to me about. I can barely hear her over the awful music. Something about dancing on live TV. Not the famous show, some other one. I just keep nodding at what seem to be the right moments. Drinks disappear. Trips to the toilet mount up. My head begins to spin. Her other friends have moved away so I'm stuck with her. Jake's got his hand on the biter's hip and he's not losing eye contact for anything. She's smiling as he talks, laughing intermittently. The palm of her hand is flat on his chest, keeping him engaged but also at bay.

Claire doesn't seem to have much left to say. She's checking her phone even more frequently, finding nothing. I broach the subject of philosophy but she screws up her face with a fake smile, apologising for not being interested or able to take the subject on. I try films but her taste is terrible. I talk about skateboarding and this engages her. She says it's like dancing. I go to the toilet again.

When I get back, Jake is in a lip-lock with the biter. I tell Claire I'm going to leave. She lunges for my hand and weaves her fingers through mine.

"No. Don't go."

"I'm drunk," I say. "I need to go to bed."

"Me too," she says, clenching my hand tighter.

Before I know it, I'm staggering down the street with my arm around her waist. She's pale and slight but it's dawning on me that she's also lithe and toned; and her face is sort of pretty once you've looked at it for a few hours. Her quietness deepens the further we get from the Student's Union. There's confusion in her small blue eyes. It's endearing because she's nervous but I've not even decided that I'm doing this. I might just be walking her home.

As we approach her doorstep I stop a few feet away, to show her I'm not expecting anything. She turns back and likes the distance I've kept. She steps up to me and leans in. I hold her upper arms and stop her for a moment. It's not that I don't like her. I just don't feel particularly attracted to her. She seems pleasant enough, but we don't click. It turns out that I'm too drunk to explain this. Her lips are right there, her skin, and a pinch of fear and humiliation is beginning to surface on her brow. I feign that I'm teasing her and lean in too.

Her kiss is a whirlpool of tongue. The term 'washing machine' comes to mind. My hands roam. Her body is firm in the right places, soft in the right places. It turns out that I want her after all, even with the overly intense kissing.

We stumble against her front door, her vodka-tinged saliva all around my mouth. She looks me straight in the eyes.

"I'm not going to sleep with you," she says.

I laugh. I'm not exactly used to the etiquette of the

circumstance but it's just about the opposite of what I expected her to say. Her right hand is beneath my hoody. The fingernails of her left hand are in my back.

"That's fine," I say. "Really."

"Come in for a drink. Mr Skater can have a drink but I'm not going to sleep with him."

I search her eyes. They flinch away. She's lost, out of her depth, alone. She smiles.

"A cup of tea would be good. Warm me up for the walk home."

We go inside and she makes tea. We sit on an old uncomfortable couch without saying much but I get the impression that she's feeling inadequate, and she's impressed with me for no real reason. I kiss her again and we end up dry-rubbing. When my hand slips beneath her top she catches it and says:

"He thinks he's getting some but he's not."

I laugh and sit up, shaking my head.

Five minutes later, when her housemate walks through to the kitchen, Claire is sitting on my lap with her knees by my hips giving me the washing-machine treatment again. I lift my eyebrows at her housemate because she's stopped to gawp at us. On her way back through, holding a steaming cup of something, pulling bite-sized chocolates from the pocket of her dressing gown, she stops to watch us again. I slip my hand up Claire's skirt and squeeze and she rolls her eyes and leaves.

My jaw is beginning to ache from the frantic kissing so I push her off me and start kissing her neck, putting my hands beneath her top. After a few minutes of the pushing and pulling game she sighs, pulls her top down, grabs my hand and tows me upstairs.

Her room lacks most of the usual late-teenage identity statements that I've become used to seeing in student bedrooms. There are two framed posters with dancers in difficult positions, somewhere between ballet and theatre, serious and intense. Everything else is monochrome and sterile. I suppose most dancers just dance, and they dance from when they're tiny and they don't do much else. This room is the result of that. The fact that it's Modern Dance that she chose perhaps suggests that there's some small urban angst in her, or a hidden emotional difficulty, because with her frame it could have been ballet, and I presume that ballet is the top dog. Then again, I'm not sure.

I turn towards her and start trying to take her clothes off. She stops me with a coy halting gesture. She has lots of little rituals that she wants to enforce. I sit on the edge of her bed while she takes her make-up off in her en suite bathroom and then puts a variety of creams on at her mirror. I'm still slightly perturbed by the fact that this eighteen-year-old has no discernible tokens of identity on display. I want to open her laptop and scroll through her libraries. And where are her books? Ebooks? At least she's mysterious on one level.

When she's finally standing in front of me, smelling like face cream and vodka, in little pink shorts and a slinky white vest, I rub the back of her legs and pull her on top of me.

"Don't look at me," she whispers in my ear after repeatedly thrusting her pelvis up and down on my groin.

I ignore her and start to take her top off. She scrambles to the light switch and turns it off. Her curtains are cheap and thin and there's a lamppost outside the window so by the time I take my clothes off I can see her in the dark. As my hands move over her I realise that I've never slept with a girl with such a perfectly toned body before. A flush of excitement flies through me. This might really be something. We fool around for a while. I put a condom on.

"Don't look at me," she says, again.

I laugh, an amused breath.

"Don't look at you? I'm inside you."

"Just don't look at me, okay?"

"Okay," I say.

I close my eyes and start pushing up into her. At some

point, I forget the rules and start looking down at her shadowy face on the pillow.

"Stop," she says. "Please. You're looking at me. I can tell."

I've only ever had slightly awkward, lusty sex; nothing too serious. A couple of girlfriends. A couple of parties. Two people desperately trying to feel something but not sure if they are. I wonder if this is how things go when you're at university. Does sex suddenly get complicated? I don't understand what she thinks is so bad about me looking at her, or admitting that this is happening, here, now.

I grind away on top of her for about forty minutes but I can't get to the point of orgasm because she keeps making her dissociative demands: "Close your eyes." "Don't look." "Turn away."

Besides her obsession with my not seeing her, she offers little else. She just lies there, inert. She moves her head instead of her body. She feels with her brain instead of her hands. While she was dressed she seemed straight forward; a bit dull but by no means odd. Now, my only point of contact with reality is knowing that I chose to have sex with her an hour ago when she was a different person.

My mind is spinning with drunkenness. This could be the only way she can get off in a one-night stand, I tell myself. Having sex with a stranger is difficult. Intimacy is difficult. It's easier to have sex with an idea. So, I try to join her world, give her the impersonal sex that she seems to want. I put my head down into the pillow and put my hand over her eyes. Her response is immediate. She reaches orgasm within ten thrusts. Since she's there, moaning, body taut and pelvis up off the mattress, I give two big thrusts and collapse on top of her.

She kisses my neck as her panting calms down. I kiss hers too then roll off her. She turns her back to me and puts her thumb in her mouth. Maybe she wants me to leave? Maybe she's ashamed? I lie on my back waiting for her to say something but within minutes I hear the change in her breathing and know she's asleep. My testicles are aching and my mind is flitting around. I look at my dark, alien surroundings and smile with exasperation. It's not that bad. Loads of guys would give anything to sleep with a girl with a body like this and here I am in bed with her, no rules or commitments, just drunken fun. She's not that weird, or freaky, or annoying. Everybody has neuroses. I just pretended to come inside her. Everything's going to be fine.

FIVE

I wake up dry-mouthed and hungover. Claire is latched onto
me, stroking my chest. She kisses me on the cheek and slips
out of bed. I fall back to sleep with an eyebrow in the air. When
she comes back into the room she opens the curtains. It's
almost winter but the sky is blue and the day is bright. Claire
has an excited spring in her ankles. With the light behind her,
her skin seems to be beaming rays that are saying, 'I can get
what I want and I've got what I want and I can keep it for ever
and ever.' Squinting, my brain pounding, I ask myself, was
she even drunk last night?

She walks towards the bed with two glasses of fresh orange
juice that she pulls out from nowhere. My immediate thought
is, *I should leave, immediately*, but this is followed by, *She
looks so good in those tiny shorts, and I'm really thirsty*. I sit
up, take the glass of juice and move over. She sits down next
to me with her legs stretched out along the bed. Her white
skin is glistening in the light. Something tells me if I reach
for her legs she'll have me exactly where she wants me. The
more appalled I become by this notion the more beautiful and
perfect her slim, toned legs seem. I last about five seconds
before my hand wanders over.

"Not in the daytime," she says, slapping my hand playfully.
"That's naughty."

I look into her small blue eyes. Is there power and manipulation hidden inside her innocence, is this how she gets what she wants, or is she really this naïve? Either way, I feel trapped and guilt ridden so I end up spending the day on her bed. We watch countless episodes of a bland emotional drama about the love affairs of Californian teenagers, all played by actors in their late twenties. Jake sends me a message saying that the biter left him high and dry on her doorstep. In my reply, I pretend I went home alone.

I'm pretty much just waiting for a moment when I feel so tense that I have to leave, but Claire is so sexy in her little shorts, and her open-sided vest reveals her neat breasts, and her tiny waist has no folds in it, even when she's sitting down, and I'm so lusty after all that build up and no release. She leans her head on my shoulder, rests her hand on my lap. Californian teenagers bicker and kiss. It gets dark outside. Claire's phone screen glows and dims, glows and dims. At some point, between a couple of washing-machine kisses, it becomes inevitable, I'm staying the night again.

When our friction becomes more pressing than the American drama, she strokes her fingertips down my eyelids, to point out that the no-looking policy is still in play. She says nothing. She closes her eyes too so I cheat and look at her. This time she's in the room with me. Her hands are on my body. Again, in a well-chosen moment, I put my hand over her eyes and she comes. Simple. And, while my hand is there, I can look at her. It takes me a while but it's just a matter of clinging to an idea: the flatness of her stomach, the curve of her hip, the bounce of her breasts. I lie with her in my arms afterwards, grateful, but I'm not sure if the gratitude is for pleasure or release. Her body feels good. That's something I can hold on to at least.

A couple of awkward, boring days go by, and then an awkward, boring week. Before I know it, I'm in an awkward, boring relationship. When I try to talk to Claire about the weirdness of the 'no looking' situation she silences me by kissing me. And I hate the way she kisses. It's like her tongue is looking for food to pick out of my teeth, writhing around, snapping and whipping. There's no intimacy, no sense that our nerve endings have found each other's and are in the tussle and play of pleasure. It's brutalist, intense friction, objects colliding and forcing gravity into the middle, where the idea of a relationship lies. There are weeks of this blind pushing and thrusting, until, gradually, my body begins to adjust to the new language, expresses it even. I stop asking questions and kiss away from myself. I put my face down into the pillow. I close my eyes.

Wiping saliva off my chin, I pick up Kant's *Groundwork on the Metaphysics of Morals*. Claire starts streaming another episode of an innocuous American drama on her laptop. I'm reading about goodwill, trying to convince myself that my adjustment to Claire's branch of intimacy is a form of benevolence. I'm trying to give her what she wants but I'm also becoming a traitor to myself and what I want. Kant would argue that this behaviour comes from a sense of duty, which means that I'm guided by reason, rather than inclination, but I know that I lack the moral worth of that argument. I'm still here, sitting on this bed, because of lust and cowardice.

Claire's phone rings.

She's always sending messages when she's watching things. She watches programmes in tandem with her friends. They have message groups for each show. They send pictures of their laptop screens to each other with little comments attached. When something 'major' happens they call each other and talk, on and on, radiation happily pouring into their brains; fictional characters, reality TV stars, simulated acts. I pretend I'm not listening, pretend I'm not irritated. Why do they never seem to meet up in real life?

"I know. And the way she waited until the reception to tell her. She's evil. I was so triggered. Do you think they'll get divorced?"

I look at her. Those slim limbs. That narrow waist. How could I want anything else? Just because she lacks a need for reality, it doesn't mean that she isn't real. Besides the weird 'no looking' rule, she seems so untroubled, so stable. Maybe I'm the problem. Maybe I'm too critical. Maybe I can't be satisfied and this is the best I can hope for. I lean over and start kissing her inner thigh. She wriggles and tries to pat me away but she's loving the attention, and the drama of not letting her excitement come through in her voice as she talks to her friend. It's almost like one of the non-events on the shows she streams.

They start discussing something else, a real person, but it veers off into a debate about a talent show and who deserves to be famous and who doesn't, and how long their fame should last; fame undoubtedly being the most valuable quality the world has to offer. I pull away from her thigh and sit up. I stare at the frozen image on her laptop screen: a beautiful American woman in diamond earrings crying on her wedding day. The phone call eventually ends.

"God, I'm so poor," she says.

She's not poor. Her parents pay her rent and tuition fees.

"Oh?" I ask, prompting her.

"Apparently, Carrie's friend, Becca, makes a hundred dollars a night streaming herself playing videogames online. Thousands of people watch her. Literally thousands. She's basically famous. They watch her play, and they click the button and give her money. Last night she did it in a push-up bra and some guy donated eighty dollars. One guy. She made nearly three hundred dollars in one night. I'm thinking about doing it."

"Dollars?"

"It's all in dollars. I don't know why."

Her vanity, her obsession with fame and being on display, is so dull, so annoying, and it sits in direct conflict with the no-looking policies of our intimate life. Her dancing, when I talk to her about it, seems to be part of a drive to get people to not just look at her but study her form. She talks about the pressure of the scrutiny, the need to make everything look perfect, never the love of movement. Now this streaming idea. Broadcasting herself so that people can look at her and validate her existence through that looking... when I'm not allowed to.

"I'm going to go out for a skate," I say. "I've got lectures tomorrow, so I'll just stay at mine."

"Kisses first," she says, in baby talk, patting her lips with her forefinger.

I put my mouth through the spin cycle, wipe the saliva off my lips and leave.

I don't go for a skate. I'm not in the mood, and it's too cold. Everybody on the streets has a pained look on their face; the depression of shortening days, the icy sting of the air. I ride my board back to the morgue and smoke weed in my room.

Jake knocks on my door around seven o'clock. I can tell it's Jake because his knock is ridiculous. When I open up he has a devious grin on his face that makes his reptilian features look both grotesque and irresistible. His hair is particularly well gelled or waxed or whatever he does to it.

"Where the hell have you been?" he asks.

"I've been around."

"You've been off the map."

"I've been at Claire's."

"Claire? Who's Claire?"

"You know. That girl from the Student's Union."

"From last month?"

I nod.

"You little butt-fucker!" he says, grabbing me and giving me a congratulatory hug. "Come on then, skin up and tell me all about it."

We sit on my bed and smoke a joint. I try to tell Jake that I've made a big mistake but he keeps ignoring my negativity, waving it away with his hands. He thinks I'm lucky. "She's a dance student, right? I bet she can bend every which way there is!" He's never been in a relationship. I can tell from his eagerness to know about mine. In the end, I just start nodding at his comments, trying not to dash his expectations.

He suggests we go out to celebrate and I agree, saying that a change of scene would do me good. He rolls his eyes and squeezes my shoulder. We drink in the Student's Union for a few hours and then get the Tube to Camden and carry on in a small alternative club called the Spider's Web. I usually find clubs loud and oppressive but I quite like this place. The toilets reek and the decor is tacky but there's something inoffensive about it all. There's no violence in the people's drunkenness. They sing and dance along to songs full of darkness and pain and wear band T-shirts from years ago. Jake says he likes it because all the girls are insecure and easy to get into bed.

I stand at a bar that looks like it's fallen out of the Marquis de Sade's imagination while Jake chats with girls. The dancefloor is full of people struggling to move in time to a Talking Heads song. The attempts of one particular David Byrne fan, hungry to prove the spiritual lineage between himself and the singer to the crowd, are keeping me amused. He's so lost and sincere.

Around midnight, sweat starts dripping from the low, black ceiling. I'm leaning against a sticky wall, sipping a bottle of beer, watching one of the goths on the dancefloor. *Everybody Knows That You're Insane* by Queens of the Stone Age is playing and, even though she's bordering on black-out drunk and the song is full of fast, chugging, distorted guitars, her dancing has a sensual brilliance to it. She's wearing a black net vest over a scarlet bra, a small black skirt, fishnet stockings and knee-high 'tear the world apart' boots. Her dancing is an alchemistic melding of archetypes; the witch, the whore, the saint... It is self-knowing and parodic, intelligent and sexual.

The longer I watch her the more a suspicion creeps in: that this dancing goth girl might be Farzaneh. But it can't be her. Farzaneh seemed too self-possessed to dress in a way that projected maladjustment or emotional pain, and too individuated to crave the shelter of a subcultural sameness. There is a sense of heightened aestheticism in her clothing though, an abstract awareness that could stretch to a form of amused fancy dress. The more I watch her the more I'm sure. It is Farzaneh. Amazing. She's amazing. You look at her but you don't see her.

A guy approaches her to try his luck. He's not a student, they're all too busy shaking their heads around. He's one of the predatory guys that comes to this place for the same reason Jake does. He dances with his hands all over her. Farzaneh looks out of control but she seems to be enjoying it. As he begins groping her, a friend, or just another girl, comes along, says something to the guy and breaks them up. As soon as he walks off and the girl turns her back, another guy, this one wearing a Motorhead T-shirt, bought on the High Street, not at a gig, swoops in for his turn. I do nothing. I can't. Not until that guy gets moved on and Jake goes in for his turn. I march over and pull Jake off her.

"What are you doing? She's fucked."

"She's fair game," he shouts, over the music. "Look at her." I don't look at her. I look at him. "Don't get soppy over some pissed bird." He's still dancing half of his body with her. "I thought you were a Manny-Manny player?"

"It's *Shaun's* girlfriend. Farzaneh."

"Nah. That's not Farzaneh."

"I'm telling you. It is."

He's smiling but his face drops when he recognises her.

"Fuck. I hope he's not in here," he says, looking around, taking a big gulp from his beer. "Cheers for the heads up."

He walks off and goes to dance about five metres away with another drunken girl in black fishnets. Farzaneh grabs my hoody. She can barely see straight. The weight of her body falls onto me. She laughs and holds onto my shoulder. The warmth of her inner thighs wraps my left leg in a confused glory. I pull her up, walk her to the bar, ask for two pints of water and sit her down at a table where the music isn't as loud.

"You should be careful," I tell her. "It's a right meat market in here."

She ruffles her lips a little, rolls her eyes and says:

"Isn't that the idea?"

"I don't know. Is it?"

"Chop it up. Put it on the shelf."

"Some of these guys though…"

"They're puppies!"

She laughs.

"Really?"

"Woof, woof," she says, with a limp hand raised, impersonating a tiny dog.

"You're wrecked."

"I'm indestructible!"

She puts her elbow on the table and rests her head in her hand.

"Nobody's indestructible," I say.

"Immortal," she mutters to herself, the beginning of a laugh slurring off into a thought.

"How much did you drink?"

Her head slides off of her hand and nearly smashes onto the table but I catch it and lift it back onto her palm. She strokes my wrist and smiles with a hazy proposition in her eyes. Eels of excitement wriggle in my arm. I pull my wrist back.

"I drank as much I wanted to drink."

"Maybe you're right," I say. "Maybe we're all just meat."

"You're a laugh a minute, aren't you?"

"Sorry."

"Look at this place," she says, slumping back onto the spine of her chair, throwing her arms out and hitting some guy in the gut. He steps away. "Look how people dress here. It's hilarious. I mean, do nightclubs even *exist* anymore? Dancing and kissing, getting too drunk. It's all so analogue. Don't you think?"

She looks amused and her speech seems lucid but her eyes are struggling to keep focus.

"It does seem like a bit of a time capsule."

"Exactly! Fucking Camden. Who are you anyway? I know you. Why won't you dance me?"

"We met at Shaun's. Here."

I push a glass of water towards her.

"Oh, you're that staring guy who smokes the weed," she says. I raise my eyebrows, trying not to agree with this description. "How come you're out and not smoking weed, staring guy?"

"I just needed to get out, and my friend wanted to come here. So here I am... not smoking weed."

She seems to think that what I've said is endearing in some way, but she rolls her eyes because she also finds endearing things ridiculous.

"I'm Farzaneh. Far-za-neh. I bet you can't spell it. Far-za-neh."

"Where's Shaun tonight?"

She scratches sloppily at some ash on the table.

"Who cares? Who cares where any of the men are?"

She tries to drink some water but almost drops the glass. I take it from her and put it back on the table.

"Can I get your number?" I ask.

"Number? Wow. You're actually, actually serious."

She rummages in her bag and gives me her phone with a haphazard gesture. I type my number in and am about to give myself a missed call when I notice a couple of her friends standing over me. The closest looks particularly vehement. I get up out of my chair.

"You shouldn't let her get like this," I say. "The guys were all over her."

"Until this chivalrous knight came along," shouts Farzanch, over my shoulder, laughing, nearly falling over the table.

A frown rises on the girl at the front. It makes her distended jaw look even more protrusive and rectangular. She folds her arms. One of the other girls rushes over to Farzaneh and stands her upright.

"She can *get* however she *wants*," she says. "I didn't see any of those other guys taking her off into a dark corner."

I nod and purse my lips.

"Phone," says the girl with the distended jaw, putting her hand out.

I'm bewildered.

"Phone," she insists.

I look down. I still have Farzaneh's phone in my hand. She thinks I'm trying to steal it.

"I was just… She said I could…"

"Phone."

I hand her the phone. She barges past me, takes Farzaneh's other elbow and walks her away with her friend.

"I know her," I call after them. "I know her."

Jake comes over while I'm watching them disappear into the crowd. He pinches my cheek and waggles my head about, laughing.

"Check you out. A girl waiting for you at home and another on the run. I knew you were a Manny-Manny player."

SIX

Time keeps getting away from me. Three months pass feeling like three weeks. It's Thursday when it should be Wednesday. It's seven thirty when it should be six. I've got the wrong books at the right lecture. I've got the right books outside the doors of a lecture that's already over. I can't seem to catch up with where I'm supposed to be. Reading is the only thing I'm doing well. My brain is hungry for information, systems, other worlds: *Ulysses*, *The Interpretation of Dreams*, *War and Peace*, *The Fall of the Roman Empire*, *Paradise Lost*. Large books. Difficult books. I just need them to be more engaging and all-encompassing than my life. When I'm reading, I'm nowhere, and everything makes sense. When I get back, I'm lost.

Day to day, I spend most of my time at university, fitting in my reading and coursework between lectures and seminars. Once I've ploughed through about seven hours of philosophy I tend to read fiction in a little café called the Blue Turtle. They play good music, the coffee is decent and the customers are young. In the evenings, I read some more and smoke weed while Claire broadcasts herself playing a computer card game called Magik Quest. Her stream is building a following. Hundreds of horny little teenagers watch her play, deriding every decision she makes and every aspect of her physical appearance in the chat bar, and she laughs and carries on and they subscribe for five dollars a month and send her one dollar donations to have their messages aired on her stream. At around eleven thirty we have sex and then go to sleep. Sometimes it seems like my life with her is a long and tedious lie, other times it feels fast and comfortable.

Sitting in the Blue Turtle, my heart is racing from my third coffee of the day. I'm reading Virgil's *Aeneid*. Aeneas is caught in the whirlpool of Charybdis. In the real world, light showers and bursts of sunshine are shifting on the ground. There is a feeling of chaotic motion in the air. The light levels keep changing. The door to the café opens in my peripherals and I glance up and see Farzaneh walking in. It's the first time I've seen her since that night at the Spider's Web. Sun is bouncing off wet surfaces in the street. Gusts of wind are blowing in past her onto my face. I pretend to look back down at my book but follow her movements over to the counter.

She sits at a table across from me with a coffee, puts her sunglasses on the table and gets out a book: *Jude the Obscure*. She has a stiff-looking black cap on that displays the words *Fuck Feelings* in shiny gold. She seems to notice me for half a second but doesn't make any acknowledgement.

Unable to focus on my reading, I keep glancing over. Her micro-responses to her book are more pronounced than most people's. Her reactions, pulled from a weightless, fictional world, are heavy in this one. I give up on my book and stare over at her. She expresses a moment of concern for Hardy's characters that stretches into horror. I feel like her face is mirroring something awful about me and my life. A doorway opens inside me. I find myself standing up and walking over to her table. My body is weightless. Farzaneh is the only real thing. She looks up from her book.

"Yes?"

"Sorry," I say, beginning to realise that this is a real event, actually happening.

"A male human being who apologises. This should be interesting."

I shift my weight from one foot to the other. I can't think of what to say. Outside, the street shifts from light to dark to light again. Farzaneh looks like she can't decide whether to be amused or offended by my presence. The length of the pause draws her towards irritability.

"So, can I help you with something or will my services as an object you want to look at be enough?"

"No. I just…"

"What?"

"I'm sorry. I'm not sure what I'm doing."

I look around the coffee shop, checking reality is still in place, thinking about walking away, but I'm stuck to the spot.

"You're objectifying me. That's what you're doing."

"No. I don't think so. I just had to… We met before, at the Spider's Web."

"I'm sure you're completely memorable," she says, her eyes moving back down to her book.

"You are," I say, blushing a little bit.

She looks up.

"You know, with guys who approach me in coffee shops, I usually just say a word like *pervert* really loud. That tends to get rid of them."

I smile and the smile sharpens my mind. I'm here, talking to Farzaneh. This is real.

"Sounds fun," I say.

"You like public humiliation? It can be arranged."

"No. I like the idea of you rejecting overconfident men in coffee shops. It's not something you see enough of."

She leans forward and looks me deep in the eyes in a searching but mildly ironic way.

"You're a bit strange, aren't you?"

"I don't think so," I say, smiling, energy in me now. "Maybe."

"Maybe?" she says, with a laugh.

"Sorry. I understand why you don't like me coming over."

"Another apology?"

"It's transparent, and it's ugly, but sometimes you have to do something, if you want to know someone."

"And you think you want to know me?"

"Yes."

"Not fuck me?"

"What? No. I mean, not that I..."

"Relax," she says, tilting her head, softening. "You've passed the moron test."

"Does that mean I am a moron, or I'm not?" I ask, wit finally surfacing in me.

She rolls her eyes.

"I see you have a skateboard over there. Isn't that something eight-year-olds do?"

"Eight-year-olds and me, yes."

"You're funny. Seriously though, didn't the cool kids stop skating about fifteen years ago?"

"There hasn't been a cool kid since nineteen-ninety-one."

She cocks her head to one side and grins.

"You talk some shit, don't you?"

"It's been said."

Beginning to feel welcome, I move to sit down.

"Don't sit. I want to see you ride it."

"You want to watch me skate?"

"Yes," she says, putting her book in her bag. "I've never really seen skating in real life. Maybe I'll be impressed."

She stands up, taking a big glug of her coffee, and waits expectantly.

"What's wrong?" she asks. "Can't you perform under pressure?"

"No. I'm just... Let's go."

She steps away from the table, leaving her coffee steaming in her cup. Things in Farzaneh's world move quickly. They happen *now*. I grab my backpack and my skateboard and follow her out of the coffee shop.

I take her to a little spot I know down the road, outside a rundown textile warehouse. There's a raised platform with a few steps and a rail, a couple of concrete blocks and a slanted ledge leading up to a loading bay. I kickflip the steps, noseslide the rail and crooked grind one of the blocks.

"You're actually good," she says.

"I get by."

After a while I forget that Farzaneh's there. I'm in the centre of myself, making urgent physical gestures and manoeuvres, forging tricks out of time and space and gravity, forcing my board to switch and flip. I've only been using my skateboard to get from A to B. I haven't skated like this in months. Pausing to breathe, taking a moment to plan my next trick, I look over at her. She's sitting at the top of the ledge in her sunglasses looking like an album cover: knees up, arms around her legs, huge rusty doors behind her. I know from experience that a frontside-flip that turns from her and sends me back down the ledge will look impressive from her vantage point so I gather some speed and skate towards her.

The trick is difficult and I rarely land it but I'm feeling bolstered by her presence. Unfortunately, my eagerness doesn't translate into muscle memory. I misjudge the pivot point, apply the wrong pressure and land with the nose of the skateboard up in my testicles. I yelp in pain, crouch down on my knees and cup my groin. When the first wave of blinding nausea recedes I look up, expecting to see Farzaneh stifling laughter, but she's serious and thoughtful.

"I never really thought about it before."

"What's that?" I ask, sitting on the back of my heels, biting my bottom lip, vision blurred.

"I see a shitty old warehouse and wonder why some rich investor hasn't come along and turned it into flats: the industrial past, the rich and the poor, inequality, society. You see all these angles and movements. It's like you're turning the city back into the natural world. Adapting to it instead of being ruled by it."

"Skateboarding definitely makes you look at things differently. I got my first board when I was four. Only a shitty little thing, but I've always had one. Sometimes walking seems strange to me. I see the world in terms of how skateable it is."

I shift around next to her, so she can't see the pain I'm trying to repress from my expressions.

"But what it stops you from seeing seems just as important as what it makes you see," she says. "I didn't realise before but it's a completely alternative way of being. It must mean that something about what's really here doesn't suit you."

"You got all this from watching me do a few tricks?"

"No. I got all this from wondering why you'd run the risk of doing that to your balls."

She smiles and the sight of joy in her face soothes me. I smile back and the pain in my testicles begins to fade.

"You make it sound as if it's about denial, but it's about seeing what's in front of you more exactly, using objects as objects, forces as forces. You're you, and you're now, and you're here."

"It's about freedom then?"

"Sometimes, thinking about skating, the idea of it being in my life, it's more powerful than actually doing it. It's like there's a light inside me. I guess you could call it freedom. It feels more like honesty."

"The really important thing is not to live," she says, "but to live well."

"Exactly. That's pretty much my mantra. I love Plato."

"You know it?"

"*The Last Days of Socrates* is my favourite book. I do Philosophy at uni."

"It's one of my favourites too. It made me cry. I used to do Philosophy. Last year. But I switched to English Lit. They let me transfer my credits."

"So, you're nineteen?" I ask.

"Twenty."

"Oh."

"Ancient, I know."

I smile and carry on:

"After saying that, about living well, Socrates argues that he should stay in prison and be put to death, not try to escape, because his freedom has been taken by the same institutions that provided it."

"I'm not sure I agree with him on that though," she says. "Freedom is bigger than society, and it's bigger than duty or integrity. I mean, it's being in-itself. And he's choosing not to be."

"Yes. When I'm reading it, I always think he should escape."

"I *know*. If I was Crito I would have just put him on my shoulder and run off with him."

"I imagine the same reasoning occurs to most skateboarders in the end; that they have to join in, work, pay their bills, because society has educated them and protected them, it's allowed them to have a certain amount of freedom, and if they want their children to be educated and protected then they have to contribute something towards it."

"What about *total* freedom? Doesn't anybody get that?"

"I'm not sure it exists."

"But different lifestyles have to be closer approximations."

"I guess. But I don't think a skateboarder is any more liberated than anyone else."

"Unless a skateboarder gets really good and plays society at its own game," she says. "Sells how good he is at being outside back to the inside. Sponsorship. Products. That way he gets to stay free."

"But doesn't that defeat the object of being outside?"

"Probably. But maybe it changes things, bringing the outside in. It moves things forward. Brings us closer to the ideal. Piece by piece."

"Yes, but it also submits to the idea that value can only be apportioned to the outside by the inside. And maybe that's just an imperialist way of stripping the outside of its meaning, by conquering it."

"That's true…" she says, taking a moment to think about this. "I wish I had something in my life that made me feel free."

"It's never too late to learn," I say, smiling.

"I'd kill myself on one of those things. I have no sense of danger."

"Then you'll probably be good. Come on."

I stand up and move down to the flat land and put the skateboard down at my feet. Farzaneh stands up and walks down the ledge with guile in her eyes. I lodge my foot beneath the board to stop it from moving about.

"Your weight always has to be over the middle," I say. "You fall when your weight isn't pushing into the centre of the earth. And when you step onto it, put your feet over the bolts, so it doesn't flip up."

She's keen to prove that she's fearless and steps on too quickly. Even with my foot beneath it, the board upends. Farzaneh grabs onto my neck and is already laughing in mid-air as she falls. I pull her back to her feet and retrieve the skateboard.

"Try again. Remember to keep your weight over the middle. If you're putting weight or pressure on the right foot you need to lean over to the left, and vice versa."

She manages to get onto the board this time. I pull her ten metres along and ten metres back. Her legs are rigid, unused to the motions. She's holding onto my arm and smiling, her eyes wide and black and excited.

"Faster this time," she says.

I pull her back and forth, faster, and she squeals as her weight fails to shift and she nearly falls. I support her and pull her back up into her centre of gravity.

"Let's try a jump," I say.

I put my foot beneath the board and tell her to jump after three. When she does, I lift the board with my foot, keeping it stuck to her feet, pushing up so she gets longer in the air. We do this four times, holding hands.

"I want to go down the ramp," she says, looking over at the loading bay.

"I'm not sure we're quite there yet. I'd have to let go of you."

"It looks fun."

"Why don't you sit on it? Like a sledge."

"No. I want to do it properly."

"If you fall it will really hurt."

"I don't care. I want to try it."

"Okay."

I take her to the top of the ramp and put the board in place, my toes in front of the wheels to stop it from rolling down. She steps onto the skateboard, over the bolts.

"It will pick up speed," I say. "You have to lean into the speed or you'll fall backwards. At the bottom of the ramp you'll have to shift your weight. If you keep leaning forwards you'll fall on your face. Lift your weight onto your back foot for a second and, when all your wheels are on the flat, shift forward and push your weight straight back down into the middle of the board. Ready?"

She's gripping my arms, smiling. She nods her head.

"Rock'n'roll," she says.

I take my foot away. She begins to roll down the ramp, not quite straight. I pursue her, anxious that she is going to fall. She's picking up speed, leaning into it, veering to the right. I continue after her. As she hits the ridge between the ledge and the flatland she tries to shift her weight but she does it too dramatically and ends up shifting too far back. Her feet come from under her, the board rolls out in front and she lands on her side and pelvis. I rush to her side.

"Shit. Are you okay?"

She sits up and cups her elbow. She's in pain but managing to control expressing it. The side of her hand is cut, bleeding down her wrist. She notices the blood and looks at me with wide eyes.

"Wow," she says. "I nearly did it. First time."

"I know."

She holds her uninjured hand out. I pull her up.

"I think I felt it. Just for a second."

"Felt what?"

"Freedom. Just between when I came off and when I hit the floor. There was a moment."

"You enjoyed it?"

"I loved it," she says, putting her arms around me. "Thank you."

She pulls away, amused and intrigued by the affection she just displayed.

"Do you want to try again?" I ask.

"God, no. I think one fall is enough for today. Let's sit on the ledge and talk some more."

I retrieve my skateboard and take it to the top of the ledge. We both sit on it, the outside of our thighs touching, and we start talking about Plato again. My phone vibrates in my pocket. I take it out, a message from Claire. I can see the first part of the text before I unlock the screen: *Just in the supermarket and wondering…*

"I think we should turn our phones off," says Farzaneh.

"Yes. Let's do that."

She takes hers from her bag and turns it off. I turn mine off. It starts to drizzle but we ignore it and sit on the skateboard and talk for hours about reality, freedom, society… wherever our minds take us. I decide to roll a joint but my papers are sodden. We're drenched. The streetlights are on. It's dark. I have no idea what time it is. I feel like I've been sleeping for months and, now that I'm awake, the flow of real time and experience is too intense to keep track of. It's another kind of dream, but one I want to be in.

When I get back to Claire's I check the fridge out of habit. There's a plate waiting for me; a salmon fillet, asparagus and boiled potatoes. Yesterday, missing this expensive gesture might have meant something. I would have to play faux-sorry for half an hour, push my hand down a little more tightly onto her eyes later on, but that was before I had something real in my life. Until today, I hadn't fully realised that I'd been closing my eyes too.

I go upstairs, loosening the key she got cut for me from my keyring. Claire is streaming on her laptop, playing her fantasy card game, talking to hundreds of boys in a low-cut top, simultaneously sending messages on her phone to her friends. She's wearing the pink shorts she wore after the first night I met her. I glance at her computer screen and take in a couple of the chat messages:

No bra confirmed boys!!!
Pro plays bitch.
We love you Dancing Mage!

"Just taking a little break," she says to her webcam, clicking a few things with her cursor. "Back in five." She turns to me. "There's some food in the fridge for you. I don't know why but I couldn't get through to you today."

I take my phone out and turn it on. Three messages come through.

"It must have turned off in my pocket."

"What's up?" she says, wondering why I'm loitering by the door.

Seeing the confusion in her eyes, it's like I'm also looking into my confused past. The whole bedroom reeks of my complacency. I can't be here anymore. I can't spend another night in this room.

"This isn't working," I say.

She shuts her laptop and pushes her phone aside.

"What do you mean? Of course it's working."

"It isn't."

"We've never even had an argument."

"We've never had a conversation either."

"We talk all the time."

"Do we?"

She gets up and walks towards me.

57

"You're just feeling a bit neglected," she says, getting down on her knees. "You need me to make you feel good."

Her hands reach for my belt. She unzips my flies.

"No," I say, pulling her up onto her feet. "Stop. What we have, this isn't a relationship."

"This is the best relationship I've ever had."

"I don't understand how you can say that. How can you not see?"

"See what?"

"I'm sorry. I don't want to... I think you're a great person."

"Just not great enough?"

"I've tried. I really have."

"You want this to work. I know you do."

"But it doesn't."

She reaches for my groin again.

"What are you doing?"

"Close your eyes. Let me show you what you feel."

I grab her wrist and move it away.

"One thing has nothing to do with the other."

"Let me make you come."

"Are you listening to me? I need you to hear what I'm saying."

She turns around and stands up, poking out her bottom and rubbing it against my thighs. There is method and poise in her movement, study and training. She looks over her shoulder.

"How is this your response?" I ask.

She puts the tip of her forefinger on her lips and works her pelvis. Her refusal to acknowledge the situation is almost working. I'm beginning to feel seduced out of my reality and into hers. Those little pink shorts. Those slim, toned legs. This strange dance performance.

"Just close your eyes," she says, closing hers.

"I don't want to close my eyes. I want to scc what I'm doing. I want to see who I'm with."

"But it's more fun in the dark," she says, rearing up against me.

I grab her shoulders and turn her around, gentle but firm, at an intimate distance but holding her away. She opens her eyes, confused, and hurt by the rejection.

"You've met somebody else, haven't you?" she says.

I look up at the ceiling. I can't deny it. It's the only honest feeling I've had since I've been in London.

"I haven't slept with anybody."

"Who is she?"

"This is about us. I haven't cheated on you."

"But you want to?"

"No. I want this to be over. It's already over. I'm not sure it ever began."

This statement gets through. For the first time since I met her, she maintains eye contact with a hardened glare. The confusion has vanished, and the hurt vanity of the rejection. She's flipped a switch and I've gone from her number one man to a piece of shit. It's scary how quickly the change comes.

"You're going to regret this. Do you know how many guys want to fuck me? I've got over eight hundred subscribers. My last Instagram picture got two and a half thousand likes. I'm a fucking somebody."

I pass her the key.

"I'm sorry," I say. "I think you're great. Really. But…"

"Oh my God. This is really happening, isn't it? I feel so unsafe right now."

"Unsafe?"

She slaps the key out of my hand onto the floor.

"Get out!" she screams. "Get out!"

I turn and leave.

SEVEN

Outside a lecture hall in the English department, I can see Farzaneh through the glass in the door. It's my third attempt at finding her. I pace back and forth, look at posters on the walls. At eleven o'clock the students start putting their books and notepads in their bags and begin to walk out. There's a lightness in my chest, knowing that she's about to appear, recognise me, talk to me. Her eyes don't disappoint. She's pleased I'm here. We're both smiling. She puts her copy of *Tess of the D'Urbervilles* into her bag and approaches me.

"You know, stalking is illegal."

"Only if you get caught," I say. "I'm stalking that girl over there but I'm using you as a decoy. She'll never figure it out."

Farzaneh's smile broadens, so does mine.

"Which one?" she asks.

"The girl with the braids and all the piercings. There's something about face mutilation. I just can't help myself."

"Okay. I'll help you stalk her, but just this once."

We start following this random girl I've pointed out. Farzaneh's shoulder is on my shoulder. Our faces are stooped down low, lit up with joy.

"There's no way a rebel this big can be a student," she whispers. "She must be part of the revolution, a sleeper agent.

I bet she's planning the upheaval of the whole educational system."

"I'm going to have to pretend I'm a terrorist to stand a chance."

Farzaneh laughs. The girl turns around and glares at us. Farzaneh grabs my arm and pulls me sideways down an intersecting corridor. We stand flat against the wall giggling. Farzaneh peeks out around the corner and whips her head back in again.

"I think we've been made."

"But if she is what we think she is, she'll run straight back to base."

"You're right. We have to keep following her. We have a duty to society."

"We could make the honours roll for this."

"For the queen!" declares Farzaneh.

We sneak back out onto the corridor and catch up to the girl again. As she leaves the building we hang back and then follow her through the grounds and off campus.

"I'm actually beginning to get interested in where she's going," says Farzaneh.

"An abandoned railway arch, I imagine. To leave a message under a brick, to tell them she's been compromised."

"Or the back of a tattoo parlour full of hackers and Guy Fawkes masks."

We walk behind her all the way to the High Street. She turns and walks into Boots.

"Oh well," I say. "Even revolutionaries need toiletries and tampons. What should we do?"

"That was fun. Maybe we should follow someone else?"

"We could go for coffee?"

"Him," she says. "The sad-looking bald guy in the anorak. Don't you think that coat's suspiciously long for a day as nice as this?"

"It is suspiciously long. And it's the queen we've got to be worried about. She's sitting in her golden chair counting diamonds, just a few miles away, all so poor people like us can feel like everything's alright, and all the while this guy's out here, hiding God-knows-what kind of anti-monarchist weaponry under his anorak. It's our duty."

"For the queen!" laughs Farzaneh.

We follow the bald guy to a sandwich shop.

"Tuna and sweetcorn?" whispers Farzaneh, as we queue to buy nothing behind him. "He's a regicidal maniac."

We follow the man to a news stand. Farzaneh butts in front of him and tells the merchant we're going to need two copies of his largest newspaper, that it's a matter of national security. The bald guy reaches over and puts the money for his *Financial Times* in the vendor's hand. He walks off and gets away while Farzaneh is opening up different newspapers to see which is the biggest, suddenly genuinely interested to find out. The man behind the counter is losing patience but he comes around, shaking his head and smiling when she pays and tells him he just saved the queen from a bald pervert.

We stand around outside a vintage second-hand furniture shop with the newspapers up over our faces, our eyes peeking out over the top. We pretend we're prospecting for terrorist threats, pointing out the most passive and wimpy people as our suspects. A fat woman pushing a pram scowls at us as she passes. We rush the papers up over our faces, hiding behind them.

"We are so incognito," says Farzaneh.

"We're basically invisible."

"And there's no way our voices could travel through paper."

"Not a chance."

Farzaneh stops smiling for a moment. Her eyes slide away and then she looks back at me with a note of seriousness.

"What do you think it means?" she asks.

"What does what mean?"

"The fact that we chose this game."

"That we're horrible people who don't consider the feelings of others?"

"No. Not that. How we've positioned ourselves. Outside, looking in. Do you think that's why we enjoy it?"

"Are you always this analytical?"

"Yes."

"Good."

We smile.

"I think that's probably got something to do with it," I say.

"Me too. I want to tell you about something that happened to me the other night."

"Okay."

"I went to this gig in Shoreditch, on my own, but the band didn't show up. After the guy made the announcement, for about five seconds, everybody was just standing there looking at the empty stage, you know, thinking, what should I do? I'm here. I've paid. But there's no music. The band aren't coming. The whole venue became this big non-event. Everybody and everything was haunted by the absence of the band. It was everywhere: in the walls, the rafters, the speakers. Obviously, people started to reflect and make decisions. They went to the staff to try to get their money back. They went to get drinks somewhere else. But I just kept looking at the empty stage until everybody had left. This guy who worked there had to come over and ask me to leave. I was in a trance. I didn't understand why until later on."

"So, what was it?"

"During those five seconds, when everybody was looking at the empty stage, I felt like they were all like me, we were all together, because they could all see the nothingness in everything. There was all this anguish, and possibility, and freedom. Their response was to get away from it as soon as possible, shift back towards the real world, because they could, but I was stuck with the nothingness. I had to just keep looking at the empty stage. That was the gig I was always going to. Do you know what I mean?"

"I think so. Sometimes, I feel like there's a distance between me and the world, something that isn't there for other people. They get to be. But I don't. I have to do something strange, like jump down seven steps on a skateboard, just to feel like I actually exist. And even that doesn't always work. Except, I don't feel like that now."

"With me?"

"Yes."

"Me too. I don't feel it either. Not now. I think that's what I'm saying."

Our eyes are fixed on each other's.

"It's good, isn't it?"

She nods. Her eyes are dilating. We're still hiding behind the newspapers. I can't even remember where we are. I want to stay behind the papers for ever.

EIGHT

It doesn't quite occur to me that my summer break begins the second I click to submit my second semester essays, but there I am in front of my laptop with three months to kill before my next lecture. I think of Farzaneh first but I send a message to Jake. It turns out that he's back in Manchester. His dad has set up an internship for him, something in the finance sector, and he's not going to be around until the end of September. I arrange to meet up with Farzaneh instead. We get stoned in Victoria Park and lie on the grass, talking about what we're going to do this summer, not realising that we're already doing it.

I manage to get a job in a nearby Italian restaurant, waiting on tables six evenings a week. The family that runs the place are all friendly and they seem to like me but I'm living for the daytimes in the park with Farzaneh. On the grass, smoking pot, reading and chatting, it feels like we're becoming a couple. After seeing each other four days in a row we agree to stop making arrangements, to just say, 'See you tomorrow.' We don't arrive at the same time but it doesn't matter. There's a place we want to get to when we wake up, a patch of grass that has become our spot.

After eight straight days of hanging out and no signs of it letting up, during a laughing fit on the grass in which we're leaning on each other and letting our limbs create a new kind of exciting friction, I move in to try to kiss her. She puts a hand up in front of my face without pulling away.

"I want to," she says, "my body is into it, but monogamy is a really big issue for Shaun. He gets crazy about it. The drama is just too exhausting. I can't deal with it right now."

"Sorry. I keep forgetting Shaun exists."

"Yeah. Me too."

"Don't you feel like you're betraying him, meeting up with me all the time like this?"

She raises her chin in contemplation.

"I don't really believe in betrayal."

I laugh.

"What? The concept or the feeling?"

"I don't prescribe to the idea of belonging to anybody. I don't think that's the way human relationships should work. And, since I'm honest about that, there's nothing I could do that would be a betrayal."

"I get your point, but betrayal isn't always about people thinking they possess each other. It's about changing the way you behave to avoid betraying somebody's feelings."

"Feelings or hang ups?"

"What's the difference?"

"I'm just saying, in my experience, people make commitments because they feel insecure, or inadequate. They want to hear you say that you care about them, and that you don't care about anybody else, because they want to know that you're afraid of dealing with existence on your own, like they are, so that they can cower away from the world with you."

"Wow."

"What?"

"That is cold," I say, flopping onto my back with an amazed grin.

"Don't you agree? As soon as you get most men alone, they start to need constant reassurance. It's not my job to shield them from reality, pretend that things don't change, or that feelings stay the same. I'm not going to go around lying about the future just so the men I like can feel less afraid or alone. I face life. I live it."

I sit up on my elbows, still smiling in disbelief.

"You can't wander from person to person without making *any* commitments though."

"Why not?" she asks.

"It's not emotionally possible, for a start."

She huffs, drops her spine down onto the grass and looks up at the sky.

"You're right. I should probably dump him. Formally, I mean. Given how he thinks. It's only fair. But he's purposefully turned it into this impossible task."

"You're one on your own, aren't you?"

"We all are," she says, looking at me with a sly grin.

Lying prone with a joint in the midday sun, reading a section of Plato's *Republic* which I've read four or five times before, Farzaneh is later than usual and I'm beginning to feel annoyed. It's been three days and she's still with Shaun. It isn't halfway through the break yet, but the height of the summer is approaching and, once that peak passes, these long, lazy days in the park will become less relaxing. We'll be able to see over the hump to the next academic term, to the shorter days, to the colder afternoons. When those things come into view there will be less imperative to make this summer about us, and I'll begin to have to admit to myself that it isn't, that I've been kidding myself for weeks.

I get up off the grass and decide to go to the skate park, but then I see her walking towards me, carrying a tote bag full of snacks and books, and all my grievances turn to nothing. Her confident stroll across the grass, the slight shimmy in her neck, the blurry smile beneath her sunglasses... when I see her I feel found.

"Where are you off to?" she asks, in a chipper cockney accent.

"I thought I'd go for a skate."

"No, no. Not today," she says, reaching into her bag and pulling out an envelope. "I've got a special favour to ask."

I knock on Shaun's door. He answers, topless, muscles bulging, his mobile phone to his ear. He nods and lets me walk in. Shutting the door behind me, I feel uneasy. It's a bright afternoon but his curtains are closed. His lamp is dim. There is thick and fresh weed smoke hanging over an old and stale ashy smell. The smoking has been going on for some time. His bedsheets are a mess. There are things on the floor – books, clothes, papers, a projector, speakers – and they look like they've been thrown around. He's pacing back and forth. His eyes are full of fury.

"Fuck," he shouts, throwing his phone down onto his bed.

"What's up?" I ask, taking a slight step back towards the door.

"That woman is an absolute mind-fuck." He rubs his temples, takes a moment to filter his rage and turns towards me. "Sorry, mate. I don't have any smoke at the moment."

He picks up his phone from the bed and turns his back to me. I'm supposed to leave.

"I'm not after weed," I say.

His mobile is against his ear again. He looks back at me, irritated.

"I don't do anything else. It's just weed."

"I know. I've got this for you. It's from Farzaneh."

I hold out the letter.

"What's from Farzaneh?" he asks, turning, his phone no longer poised.

"This."

He looks down at the envelope with disdain.

"Why the fuck are *you* bringing *me* a letter from *my* girlfriend?"

"She asked me to."

"Why did she ask *you* to?"

"I don't know. She just asked, as a friend…"

He steps towards me so he's less than a foot away. Small balls of saliva have formed in the corners of his mouth. His broad chest is dank with sweat.

"And since when were you friends? Since when did you become her personal, private postal service?"

"I just—"

"Did you fuck her?"

"What?"

"It's a simple question."

"No. I just said—"

"Did, *you*, fuck, *her*?"

His voice is beginning to quiver with anger. Little bombs of foam are sputtering out with his words. He has veins popping out of muscles in places where I have dents.

"No. I told you. No."

I have pins and needles in my armpits. My face is burning. *Nothing can harm a good man either in life or death*, I think, trying to reassure myself, but at this exact moment I'm not convinced that Socrates was right about that.

"But you want to, right? Look at you," he says, stretching out his huge right arm in disbelief. "You're nothing."

He takes another step forward, grabs my T-shirt and backs me up against the wall. His damp, angry breath is lingering on my forehead.

"Tell me the fucking truth," he says.

"Honestly, I just said I'd give you the letter."

"What? While you were talking about how messed up I am?"

"No. Nothing like that. She just asked if I'd do it."

"Fucking bitch," he shouts, releasing me, snatching the letter from my hand. "She's the one that fucked this up. A letter. Who sends a fucking letter?" He stops and scowls at me. "Just… *sit down*."

I look around at the mess everywhere, move over to his bed and perch on the edge.

"If I sense your dick, in any way, in any fucking word of this, you're never going to leave this room. Do you understand?"

"Yes, but—"

"Shut up."

He sits at his desk. I'm staring at his door, wondering whether to make a bolt for it, but I decide it will be best if I stay where I am. He opens the letter and begins reading. Within seconds his neck has sunk deep into his shoulders and he's absentmindedly rubbing his head. I sit in silence trying to anticipate his response, anything to get away unharmed.

As he turns the page, he begins emitting an almost visible sorrow. By the time he's on the final passage, he's trying his hardest not to cry, but holding it back is making his shoulders judder. I can't imagine what coded mix of words could bring this mountainous, aggressive man to weep. I don't know what to do. My instinct is telling me to comfort him but I know better than that. I sit and wait.

When he's finished reading he gently places the letter down on his desk. He takes a few slow, deep breaths, then stands up and allows his chair to fall back onto the floor. Head down, he walks to the opposite wall where his sink is, looks up, stares at himself in the mirror and then punches the glass three times, powerfully and methodically. The mirror cracks on the first punch, breaks on the second and shatters into the sink on the third. The silence in the room, after the power he has exerted, makes the space seem empty and broken. He puts his hands up on the wall, on either side of where his mirror used to be, and drops his head and neck down.

Thirty seconds pass before he remembers that I'm in the room. He turns in my direction, looking like he's been hurt so badly that he could have done nothing but punch a mirror to smithereens. He stumbles backwards away from me and slouches down onto the floor, sitting with his knees up beneath his sink. The knuckles on his right hand are bleeding. His mouth is grimacing, producing the effect of a silent wail. I have to say something.

"Can I—"

"Don't look at me," he says, snapping back into himself. "Get out. Don't ever come back."

I stand up and leave the room, squinting as the sunlight floods the space around me.

Back at our spot in Victoria Park, Farzaneh looks up at me expectantly. I nod to let her know it's done but also hunch my shoulders to show that I'm a little bit shaken up by the experience. She stands up, relieved and excited, pulls me to her and kisses me. The lengths of our bodies connect. Our lips are symbiotic; just the right amount of movement, no gaps for air, no teeth, no tension in our tongues. I'm lost in her.

She pulls back and looks at me as though playfully warning a child.

"Don't get any ideas," she says.

"What do you mean?"

"I express my moment. That's all."

"Okay."

"You're a pretty good kisser."

"Thanks," I say, bewildered. "You too."

NINE

Downstairs at the old morgue, Kant's *Critique of Judgement* has arrived in my postbox so I decide to head to the park a few hours earlier than usual. The first module on the second year of my course is on aesthetics, art and beauty, so I'm keen to read his take on the agreeable, the beautiful, the sublime and the good. I'm still enjoying the feel and smell of the new book when Farzaneh turns up, also early. As she walks towards me, between the air and the line of her body, there is an ecstatic fuzz. It's hard to see her edges. Something in the centre of her is smiling. She skips up next to me with a bounce, leans down, kisses me, then pulls her face back a few inches and looks over her sunglasses straight into my eyes.

"Thank God for you," she says.

"What are you doing here so early?"

She grabs my hand and attempts to pull me up.

"Let's go."

I resist and try to pull her down.

"Go where? The grass is just starting to warm up."

"I've got a surprise."

She pulls back at my hand with both of hers, a parody nag that is no less determined in its effect than a real nag.

"I suppose Kant can wait."

I scoop up my bag and skateboard, clutching my book to my chest.

"I like how self-contained you are," she says. "Reading in the park. Going out skating on your own. Never too needy. So many men have nothing they're into. Shaun had his whole gym thing, and he liked films, but he basically spent most of his time fixating on me. It was the worst kind of boring."

"Has he been in touch?"

"How can he want me back? When he fucked me it was like I was a million miles inside myself. Maybe I'm a crypto-fascist or something, but idiots can't make me come."

"I know what you mean," I say, trying to smile, trying to imagine that she means that I could make her come. "My sex life with Claire was like being in a weird dream."

"Exactly," she says, getting excited. "It's like being a ghost in your own body."

"It's horrible."

"I think it's compulsive solitude. At least for me. It's like I'm watching my body go through the motions of having a good time, while knowing that I can't be having a good time, because this guy doesn't know my secret, that I'm not really there. If he knew, he wouldn't feel involved. He'd know that my body was lying, and that I was watching from somewhere else. And if he can't find my nothingness and pull me out of it, if he can't unite my being and help me experience truth, then he doesn't deserve me. He doesn't deserve to have everything that I am."

"It sounds like chronic sincerity."

"Or chronic insincerity."

"I'm not sure there's a difference."

She grabs my wrist and swings me out of the park gates and onto the street. I keep hold of her and pull back as we spin in a couple of circles before facing forwards and walking.

"What's it like for you?"

"Similar," I say. "It usually starts with me thinking something like, 'Where is she? Why is she not here?' and then that trails off into, 'But if I'm thinking like this, I'm not here either. So, where am I? Why am I not here? Where is this happening?'"

"Brilliant," says Farzaneh, laughing.

"Then there's this fight to get back into my own head, or to get out of my head, to focus on the physical, but the physical is all happening in my head, so I can't get near it."

"You sound even more fucked up than I am."

"It's not all the time."

"No. It's not all the time for me either. But when it isn't, when I just plunge into it all, it's usually for me, because I need something to be felt and true. It's like a drive. It's not about connecting with the guy. It's about connecting with myself."

"It's all so messed up, isn't it? What's the evolutionary imperative to have brains like these?"

"God knows," she says, clenching my hand. "Sometimes I wish I was just a normal person who could believe everything was real."

There is a sense of spinning and joy and light between us, like we're finally taking the physical journey that has so far only been imagined. I'm clinging to the idea that she is taking me to her place. A guarded treasure. Somewhere I know Shaun was never invited.

"So," I say, "do you think it's just people like us who can't connect with other people or do you think that other people can't either but they just don't know they can't?"

"Oh, I'm definitely in the solipsistic camp."

"In your world, when people share a connection, it's just a shared delusion then? When it happens, it's because both people are imagining that what's happening is deep and sincere at the same time."

"I guess."

"What about love?" I ask.

She lets go of my hand, rolls her eyes and sighs as though this 'love' obstacle is always getting in her way.

"Why wait for some fairy tale to come along and save you?" she says, doling out what is clearly the start of a preconceived rant. "Why not just accept yourself as you are and accept your journey as it is? People talk as though love is separate from the emotional spectrum. Even though they know from their own experiences that it's not permanent or all encompassing, that it comes and goes as it pleases, they cling to this narrative that it's the end point of all personal accomplishment, that it will complete and unify them, that it will last forever."

I smile because it doesn't feel like she's pre-emptively rejecting our love. It's more like she's trying to broaden my emotional expectations, raising my sights, telling me what a relationship with her could be about.

"People do need it though," I say, nonetheless accepting my place on the other side of the argument. "Sharing something true with someone else, and having that truth last, it gives people a sense of meaning and purpose."

"Love isn't about sharing something true," she says, looking at me as though I should know better. "Love is just a myth people use to justify their fear of freedom. It's also a form of narrative control, a Christian hangover, keeping women pure and monogamous to protect the male ego."

"That's deeply cynical."

"Okay. Let me put it another way. Love is subjective. It's locked inside a brain. Imagine a couple where a woman is full of hero-worship and hope for the future while her lover is full of lust and excitement about the present, if they never bothered to explain what they were feeling in any detail, if they both called it love, they would both probably think they were experiencing the same thing. They'd be making a commitment based on a complete misunderstanding."

"But, even if the moment by moment experience differs, if love makes two people feel connected to each other, what's to say they're not?"

"I'm not saying they're not. I mean, everything *is*

connected. But there's nothing magical about that. Love isn't some mystical force pairing off souls that were pre-ordained to meet. Love is everywhere, you can find it in anyone, because it's inside you. Your relationship with love is just your relationship with yourself."

"What if everything aligns? What if two people are meeting on the same level, and their internal processes mirror each other's, they trust each other, they act on that trust, they become monogamous, they value that exclusivity, that person. What then? Isn't that meaningful?"

"Not really. It's just a happy coincidence. That stuff never lasts long before it's all out of sync. The trouble is nobody talks about how dysfunctional monogamous relationships really are. We feel ashamed to because we're told so often how the narrative of it all goes. The only people who are any good at love are the idiots who just keep regurgitating and reinforcing the same emotional narrative long after the intensity of the feelings have simmered away."

"Your world scares me," I say, "but you're pretty amazing."

"Yes, I am," she says, smirking, grabbing my hand again.

"Let's turn the road into an obstacle course."

"Okay."

I jump up onto the garden wall we're walking by. She clambers up behind me. We walk along with our arms out, climb a brick turret, step across two gaps over gates and make it onto the next garden wall. A bush nearly pushes us off but we make it to the gatepost. The next jump is wide and difficult but skateboarding has prepared my legs. I make it. Farzaneh won't risk it but she seems impressed at my daring. I scramble across a few more walls but it's not as fun without her. I climb back down and step onto my skateboard. She holds my hand and pulls me along, flinging me around the corners.

"Here we are," she says.

"Yes, we are."

"No. This is my house."

"This whole house?"

"Yes, I own a whole London townhouse."

"Seriously?"

"No, not seriously. I rent a bedsit on the first floor."

She kisses my cheek. I look around. It's in a pleasant part of Tower Hamlets. There are trees on the pavement.

"It's nice around here."

"I know."

"Isn't it funny that trees make you feel like you're less likely to get stabbed?"

She smiles.

"Especially since they're perfect objects for attackers to hide behind."

We enter the building and walk up to the first floor. Her room is huge. The double bed barely takes up a fifth of the floor space. Her walls are covered with the thickest bricolage of images and words that I've ever seen. There are quotes with all kinds of non-European names I've never heard of beneath them, poems ripped from books, small, page-sized stories with strange little illustrations, scratchy, expressive paintings, rants in angry handwriting, bold and abstract statements, defaced articles clipped from newspapers and magazines, postcards from galleries, flyers from obscure underground events, tickets from equally obscure gigs, strange little objects. It's impressive, and a little nuts.

There are two internal doors: one leads to a bathroom and the other to a tiny kitchen. Lots of clothes and pieces of paper lie around on the floor and there are piles of books everywhere. Hippy throws are pinned up, rounding off the ceiling's corners. A bunch of hand-made Persian sheets are strewn across her bed.

I start reading a handwritten poem on the wall closest to me. It's on midnight blue paper and there's a chalked crescent moon in the top right corner. I manage to read, *Before, when you pulled the oceans through me / And time, and space, and blood*, but then she pulls me away to the middle of the room and holds my hands so that I have to face her and stare into her eyes.

"I want to tear everything down," she says.

"Why? It looks great in here."

"I thought you could help me."

Looking around at her intricate collage of art and information I can't help but feel that it's a waste, not to mention a bizarre way to treat your own creative projects, but since she's finally brought me into her private space I feel obliged to be convivial.

"If you like," I say.

She nods and kisses my cheek.

We peel everything away from the walls and roll all the Blu Tack into one big ball. Every time I try to read something her hand is over it in a second, tearing it away. In the end, I stop trying and do the job in hand with as little curiosity as I can muster.

When we're done and there's a little mountain of paper in the middle of the room Farzaneh pulls down a huge suitcase from on top of her wardrobe and stuffs it all in. It's already half full with scraps of paper and random objects. She has pasted a sign that ironically reads *baggage* onto it at some other point in time. After she's packed all the stuff away she smiles at me.

"Now we can start from scratch," she says. "You go first."

She grabs a black pen and a piece of paper from her desk and passes them to me. I sit on the edge of her bed and try to think but nothing occurs to me. I'm too excited, increasingly aware that this is the start of a new phase, that this moment is important. Farzaneh puts her arms around me and starts shaking me, egging me to hurry up. When she stops I put pen to paper and write out an idea:

An anti-corporate product succeeding in a corporate economy does not mean that capitalism will build the weapons of its own destruction, it means that capitalism can sustain freedom and is a vehicle for ideological evolution.

"A message of hope for the disaffected youth," she says, scrunching up the paper and throwing it at her overflowing waste paper bin. "How adorable. But I don't want a message. I want you to express something."

I laugh. She's right. I just wrote it to seem clever, an anti-rebel.

"Let's just wait until it happens naturally," I suggest.

"Nothing happens naturally. Everything has a decision behind it."

"Okay. How about this?"

I write out something that comes from nowhere:

These are not the words you're reading.

"Perfect," she says.

She gets up and sticks it to the wall. As she turns back towards me she gets down onto her hands and knees. My stomach lifts as she crawls by me but she shuffles to the side with a mischievous grin and reaches under her bed.

"Are you ready for the surprise?" she asks.

She passes me a baggie full of large, Mexican magic mushrooms. They have bright orange caps speckled with tiny silver flakes and beige/brown stems.

"I've never done mushrooms," I say.

"Me neither."

"I don't know. I'm a bit scared of having a bad trip. My imagination can be a bit dark sometimes."

"If the deepest recesses of your mind have got something scary to say you should be listening to them."

"Maybe."

"Look at it this way, we both enjoy exploring ourselves and our ideas, and what could be a more intense version of that than seeing your brain spilling out in front of you?"

"You're serious, aren't you?"

She nods.

"Okay. Fuck it. Let's do it."

"Shall we eat them or make tea?"

"Tea?"

Farzaneh boils the mushrooms in a pot of water with some spices and pours the tea into cups.

"I made a hallucination-themed playlist," she says, putting 'White Rabbit' by Jefferson Airplane on.

We sit on her bed and start sipping the mushroom brew.

"How long do they take to kick in?" I ask.

"About twenty minutes, I think."

"I'm nervous."

"There's no one I'd rather do this with."

"You're the only person I'd do this with."

We finish our drinks and sit back against the headboard. The changes are small to begin with; a need to stretch my arms and legs, less contrast in my vision, an ease in weight and gravity.

"Do you feel anything?" I ask.

"Almost. You?"

"Same. I'm glad we're doing it here. I like your room."

"I'm glad too."

We lean in towards each other and kiss, closing our eyes. A chasm opens between our mouths. Thousands of tiny crevices on the surface of her tongue open a grassy field of magenta in my mind. Her lips are clouds, limitless sky. I'm laughing. Farzaneh is laughing. Our kiss has ended without my noticing the division. We're holding each other but our limbs are not flesh and our bodies are boneless. We are gases passing through a oneness, together.

"Open your eyes," I say, after opening my own.

"How is this possible?" she asks.

Music dances in the air between us, fluorescent orange and gold. It washes over Farzaneh and through her and then lifts into a sky above her baggy white shirt which is now a sprawling alpine mountain range. My arm, stretching out towards it, attempting to check the principles of the landscape's reality, becomes a fusion of hexagons that spin off into a strange weather system.

"I'm really into you," I say, and the words form land and air around the mountains.

"I'm really into you," she says, and her words are orbs of white light hanging in suddenly sprouted black trees in the foothills.

The purity of the trees' fruit, and her words, expands and passes into me; sight, sound and meaning, all one.

"We're lucky," I say. "Don't you think?"

"Yes," she says. "We really are."

I journey towards one of her black trees, amazed by its existence, a shadow on a thread of cotton lurking behind it, particles of light as the fruit. A soft crease forms a path along a mountainous crevice. Lemon music clouds drift in the air above an orchard on her legs. The orchard stretches for miles, little white lights in all the trees, the whole bed a vast wilderness.

To the left, in the west, a great precipice stands tall, a chest of drawers, clothes spilling out into waterfalls of red and green, and a special tree at the top. It has the most beautiful of all the fruit, the brightest of white lights. Farzaneh is up there, caught in the vision, implicit in the tree. A reflection on a hairdryer? A pile of hair bobbles? What used to be there doesn't matter. Just the perfect black tree with the fruit made of light.

"My arms are so long," she says.

Two thick branches covered in white fruit stretch out over the forest. I pluck an orb off a branch and it dissolves into my hand and sends spasms of ecstasy up through my arm.

"You're inside me," I say.

"I know," she says, weaving her fingers through the musical clouds, creating a watery yellow wave that flows out through the room. "You're inside me."

We draw close and hold each other, laughing with joy, and the sound leaves our mouths as a flock of bright green parakeets, flying in perfect accord above the forest, up and away, across the gleaming turquoise curtains. *How can this be?* I wonder. And the question reignites the gleam of the white fruit in the trees, a hundred thousand lights which hold a hundred thousand hopes, and the feeling of all that hope floods in through my eyes without words.

"I know how to believe," I say.

"Me too," says Farzaneh.

"You're the light in the trees."

"You're the ripples on the water."

We laugh and the colours shift. I see Farzaneh's water rising above the trees. The fruits are glints of light on the tips of waves and ripples. The glassy wetness is dispelled by the hand on the end of my mile-long arm, not feeling water but a fission of scratchy threads and tiny snapping branches. The vision settles into a mix of bed sheets and Persian throws, the lines of the patterns and weaves moving and shifting. The mountain in the west is a chest of drawers. I look back at Farzaneh. Her face shimmers and glows.

"Is it just because we're high? Will you say you're into me tomorrow?"

"It's the truth," she says. "We're not afraid of the truth anymore."

"We never have to be afraid of the truth again."

"Never."

"Let's promise."

We shift to face each other and join hands, cross-legged on the bed. Farzaneh's eyes are cosmic events.

"We'll always be honest," she says, and the words drift into the chasm between us, her water returning and rising, the breeze in her sentiment forming the ripples on a vast lake.

"We'll always be honest," I say, my words adding depth to the water, while the purple mist of a song which I think might be by Royal Trux floats and shifts above the surface.

I look across the great lake, sure that Farzaneh is looking back across the same one, so sure that I don't need to confirm it. I believe it. We are melting into each other's imaginary landscapes, moonlight rippling on a body of water that we know there isn't space for and definitely doesn't exist.

"Do you see…"

"Yes…" I say.

"Between us."

"Yes."

"I see it too."

"I can feel the weight of it all."

"Me too."

"I can feel the whole thing. Even the bits that must be you."

"It's so trippy."

"Are we being ridiculous?" I ask. "It feels so real."

"It feels like the only real thing that's ever happened."

"We're part of the same world."

"Joining together."

"I'm really into you," I say, again.

"I'm really into you," she confirms.

"Those words feel so good."

"They feel amazing."

"How do words feel?"

A hundred thousand pure white lights gleam beneath the surface of the lake. I gasp and shiver and stare into the centre of the centremost light, and all the lights are one light, and all the words are one word, and that light and that word are part of the same vision, and that vision is an eye that looks out from inside of everything.

"I wish I could keep what I know now," I say. "The way I know it now."

"It was already inside us. We just opened it up."

"How can we make so much sense when everything's like this?"

"I don't know," she says. "I love our brains."

"I love our brains too."

We laugh.

"Shall I skin up?"

"God, yes."

"What are we going to do about this?"

"Let's open our arms and let it disappear."

"Okay."

We release our hands and open our arms and the lake spills out around us. At the edge of the bed I reach into a long corridor version of Farzaneh's room and pull a faraway table up to my wriggling knees. Rolling up, the tobacco is a cactus to my fingertips, the table is a desert planet in another dimension, the floor is a bottomless abyss. It takes a long time, feeling with the back of my brain, decoding the shift of worlds, but the joint is eventually ready. We roll around together on the floor, shivering with joy as we smoke it, everything swirling in motion. Somewhere, in the middle of it all, Farzaneh says:

"I'm going back to the other world now."

"The diamonds are electric," I reply.

By the time I wonder what time it is, over six hours have passed. It takes me about four attempts to see the digital numbers on the screen of my phone. When the numbers finally stay still and make sense, I become confused by the concept of time as something linear, broken up by food and lectures and shifts in the restaurant. I'm not sure I want to return to it.

"Wow," says Farzaneh, coming around. "That was unbelievable. Are you beginning to level out too?"

I nod.

"I'm so horny," she says. "I feel like my skin is fucking my clothes."

She reaches down beneath her bed. When she stands up she's holding a white Venetian mask. It's elaborately decorated with purple gems around the cheeks and eyes. It has twisting gold and silver lines on the face and shiny purple feathers extruding from the forehead and around its sides. She puts it on. A hallucinatory wave turns the mask into a moon in a sky full of moving colours. I focus, pushing through the distortion.

"My dad bought me this mask," she says. "When I was eleven. After my mum died."

"Your mum died?"

"She killed herself."

"That must have been terrible."

"She didn't want to be here. You're the first person I've told in London."

"What was she like?"

"She was quiet. Then she was loud. I used to think she was scary. I'm not sure what she was."

"I can't imagine."

"Since I'm getting real, I should probably tell you that my dad died too. Two years ago. Cancer."

"Shit. That's awful."

"The only good thing about having dead parents is that I'm basically rich, after the sale of the house."

"I guess, but—"

"I don't want sympathy. I just want to explain the mask in a way it can be understood."

"Okay. Sure."

"My dad took me to Venice, a couple of months after Mum died, when things were less intense. He took me to a shop full of these things and told me to choose the most beautiful one I could see. After I picked it out, we went for a ride in a gondola. He took the mask out of the bag, pulled off the paper and fastened it to my face. With his hands around mine, leaning across the boat, he told me that I would never feel the same, and that things would never get any better, but that I would become incredibly strong, more able to carry it each day, and that a tragedy makes a young person ready for the world."

She begins unbuttoning her shirt, revealing a black bra. I shift a little. My head is spinning. Suicide? I want to know more but I daren't ask. I don't know if lust is appropriate right now. But this is about her revealing herself. She wants me to know, before we're intimate together. This is important to her. I'm important. The mask gleams white. Speckles of light dance around it.

"I wore the mask the whole time I was there. People kept jumping out of their skin, catching sight of me out of the corner of their eyes. I felt as though I'd disappeared and been replaced with something more powerful. That was when I was beginning to understand who I was, who I was going to be."

"And who was that?"

"Somebody with too much beneath the surface. Hidden by my face, and my body, unknowable, and so free."

"I don't understand."

She undoes the button on her jean shorts and slips them down over her hips.

"You can never show somebody who you are," she says. "Or what you've been through. The body is a mask. You just have to show people your moment."

"Your moment," I say, "you've mentioned that before."

Farzaneh is down to her underwear. Plain, black cotton. Inviting curves. The white Venetian mask is throbbing, pounding my eyes. She is attempting to reveal her deepest self, not just her body. I'm longing to touch her but I feel like, if I do, she might disappear, I might find myself floating on the other side of the universe.

"Want me to leave it on?" she asks, leaning over me, pulling my T-shirt off from above my head. "I could be your Venetian goddess."

"No," I say, smiling. "I want to see your face."

She slips the mask off, hangs it on a nail on the wall and joins me on the bed. I pull her towards me, desperate to feel her skin against my own, both of us naked in seconds. My fingertips move across her clitoris and her pelvis surfs over an ocean of pleasure. Perhaps the mushrooms are still having an effect but she is extremely touch-sensitive. There is no hint of distance in her. She squirms and writhes. Her face scrunches and scrunches and then her body stretches out, spasms and becomes taut. Her mouth forms a perfect circle and a note of sensual gratitude rises up to the ceiling from deep inside her. Her climax is long and graceful and she falls from it with shivers of appreciation.

"I want you inside me," she whispers.

I almost reply with the same statement before realising it doesn't apply and instead grab her and twist her down onto the bed beneath me, months of desire unleashed. The sex feels loose and free, soft and wet, almost frictionless. I'm part of an ancient dance, a deep synergy of self and other. No thoughts. No reflections. Just motion, energy, sensation, release. We come at the same time and lie back. My mind is in meltdown with blurry joy.

"That was, I don't know what that was," I say. "I never thought it would feel like that for me."

"I feel so free," she says.

"Me too."

"Want to play a game?"

"What kind of game?"

"Easy, just answer… When we rule the world, what will we do?"

"Erm… When we rule the world we'll go Bill Hicks on everyone. We'll ban defence budgets and corporate profits, stabilise every nation, invest in technology and then we'll get the hell off this planet."

"Fuck that," she says laughing. "When we rule the world we'll kill everyone who hasn't read Plato and the Sophists."

"And we'll give chavs and Tories vasectomies at sixteen."

"Castrate them at twelve more like."

"Then we'll legalise all the drugs that come from the earth."

"Everything comes from the earth," she says laughing, tapping me on the forehead.

"Okay, we'll legalise everything."

"Everything!" she exclaims, laughing.

I pull her towards me and we get back to finding out about each other's skins. It's hard to tell where I end and she begins. We have no edges. Objects are behaving like waves lapping together and over each other. Passion unfurls for pleasure and pleasure releases passion; tasting, holding, moving, laughing. We glide up into another shared orgasm and then lie on our backs.

"Do you ever feel like your fingers don't really reach the ends of your fingers? Like you've got little baby hands inside your real hands?"

We're smoking a joint. Our central arms are touching and skyward. We're intertwining and playing with our fingers.

"All the time," she says, as if this is a normal question. "Sometimes I have to squeeze something to take the edge off. And I always curl my toes up."

"I do that too."

"It's a sign of a sensitive nervous system," she says. "That's what I think anyway. In the fingers it means you should be doing something creative and in the toes it means you should be doing something active. You need to learn to listen to your body."

"I will," I say, pausing to listen to it. "I think I should be doing something creative."

"Me too."

We get up, naked, wrap our arms around each other, kiss, laugh and feign thinking noises. Holding each other close, we step around in circles to music that isn't there.

"Let's paint," she says all of a sudden.

"Perfect. What shall we paint?"

"Each other."

"Okay."

And we do.

We put old newspapers down and she gets out a collection of poster paints. I put a handprint on the wall and then she puts a handprint inside it. Hers being smaller, it looks like what we described earlier about fingers feeling like they don't reach the end of our hands. I tell her this.

"Deep," she says, unable to keep a straight face, bursting into laughter.

"I think we're still high," I say, laughing with her.

Next, I paint her breasts: one red, one yellow. I give her bright white nipples. We print them on the wall. I hold them pert with paint dripping between my fingers. Once a few pairs are scattered about on the walls she tells me to stand still with my arms out, facing the wall. I do as she says and she whips lots of different colours over me, eventually leaving an empty print of me on the wall.

I paint the base of my feet blue, make her lie down and print my feet on her buttocks. I massage gold into her back and hair. Before long we're having sex for the third time. We have fun, trying to push each other up against the walls so that we leave little paint prints and smears everywhere; a set of gold shoulder blades here, some multi-coloured buttocks there.

She lies on top of me exhausted afterwards, both of us shivery and twitchy. We lie in the middle of the floor for so long that the paint dries. The left sides of our chests get stuck so tight that we feel skin ripping as we try to part them. We have to walk three-legged to the bathroom, carefully but amused, and run a bath and climb into it together.

Once we're separated by the hot water Farzaneh lights some candles. We lie back. The heat in the water reinvigorates some of the psychotropic sensations. I drift out from my body into a warm fog. Farzaneh is in here with me, mingling and nebulous. Time stretches on and on, beyond itself.

"Not many people have had a day like this."

Her voice locates me. I shift back into my body. I have bones and limbs, a skull. The bath water is lukewarm. I run my hands up and down her stomach, over her breasts.

"Probably not," I say, with a smile.

"I think everybody should do magic mushrooms at least once in their lives."

"I think it should be mandatory."

"Okay. Once a year."

"Once a week."

She laughs.

"I feel like today was important."

"Me too," I say.

"We could go anywhere from here. Anything could happen."

PART TWO

ONE

I clatter along the pavement full of adrenalin. My skateboarding has taken an upward turn. At the open-air bowl in Victoria Park I've been getting the highest airs and pulling off the trickiest and longest grinds. Today, the frontside flip finally clicked into place. My muscles accepted it, allowed it in. On flat banks, over spines, up and back down into ramps. The long-elusive trick. The one my feet could never quite catch. Caught. I feel rooted in the centre of my gravity. There is no gap between my body and mind, no space between me and the rest of the world, no negation between my feelings and my expressions. Three months with Farzaneh and all is one.

I've managed to keep my room in the old morgue for a second year. The drawback is that, to stay there, I have to become a student warden; someone on a bunch of online contact lists that first year students can access and use for help and advice. I filled in the form while convincing myself that nobody contacts the wardens. I didn't even know student wardens existed until I looked into it. The only thing I'm even nearly worrying about is the fact that every module on my course now counts towards my final degree mark so I've cut down my shifts at the restaurant in order to get ahead on the reading.

Twisting my skateboard sideways and leaning back, I powerslide to a screeching stop outside Farzaneh's house.

This is usually enough to prompt her to come to the window and drop the key out for me, but she doesn't appear. The sun is so bright that my eyes are leaking but it's not warm. A chill is creeping through the light, defying it. There is a queen bee flying by the gatepost in a confused state, barely buzzing, searching for her death bed. I pop up my board and head to the door.

The girl who lives downstairs – a Japanese foreign exchange student who wears John Lennon shades and black-and-white stripy tops – is leaving the house. Having seen me with Farzaneh two or three times her face flinches into an awkward snarl (which, for her, is what passes as hello). I nod and she leaves the front door open for me.

Upstairs, in the hallway, I knock on Farzaneh's door but there's no answer. I turn my head and listen. There's no sound but I have the distinct impression that she's in there. I knock again. Nothing. No sound or movement. But I know she's home. Her existence is a sensation in me. Proximity to her body fills a gap in my usual senses.

"Farzaneh?"

My hand hovers over the doorknob, makes contact. I twist and push. The door isn't locked. I open it and step into the room. The curtains are drawn, it's dark, but I can smell her. The scent is too strong to be the lingering remains of her presence. Her exhaled breath is in the air, the warmth from her chest, the musk of her body. I take another step forward.

"Farzaneh?"

Moving from the lit corridor into the dark room, my vision is cloaked. I hear a noise, something indistinct but definitely from Farzaneh's throat. I'd know her noises anywhere. Shadows form and morph in the darkness. Notions of objects begin to emerge, but nothing looks the same. The shapes are different. There's stuff all over the floor. Farzaneh's silhouette is slouched in the middle of the room.

"Farzaneh? What's going on? Have you been robbed?"

"In a way," she whispers.

"What's wrong? What's happened?"

I reach for the light switch.

"No," she calls out. "No light. Shut the door."

I close the door behind me and turn towards her.

"Are you hurt? Has somebody hurt you?"

Amorphous objects shape into possible chairs, possible shelves of books. Something white and circular is floating in the centre of the room. There's clutter on the floor. The dark masses begin to form a Gothic cityscape in my eyes. I squint and lean forward, trying to see what the white thing is, the faint moon above the black world.

"I don't want to be me anymore," she says.

"What? Why not?"

"I don't want to exist."

"You don't mean that."

"I'm not me anyway. What's the difference?"

"Of course you are. You're you."

I inch closer to the false, dim moon, stepping on something. Clothes? The sudden appearance of eyeholes in the floating white object, the presence of a face, makes my stomach lurch. I step back, but then understand what it is. Farzaneh is sitting in the dark wearing her white Venetian mask.

"Freedom," she says. "That was all I had. Now it's gone."

I kneel. My right knee catches the edge of a book. I reach to move it and my hand moves through soft wires and finds no book. My eyes search for the outline of Farzaneh's body but all I can see is the mask.

"What is this? What's going on?"

"I tried to sleep with somebody, have sex, with somebody else, but I couldn't. My body wouldn't do it. I was all caged in. I had to throw him out."

"You tried to sleep with somebody? Who? Did he do this?"

"I was free. It was the only thing I had. And now I'm trapped. My body is trapped."

I try to move past the idea of this other man, attempt to understand what she's saying and where it's coming from.

"You're not trapped."

"I used to be limitless. Now, I'm just a mess."

"This is too much. You're freaking me out."

I get up and walk over to the wall.

"No," she says. "No light."

"I'm not sitting around in the dark while you tell me about how you tried to cheat on me. You can look me in the eyes."

I turn on the light.

Everything we created and put on the walls over the last three months has been ripped down. Piles of books have been ravaged, clothes have been strewn and flung, rugs and bedsheets and blankets are tossed and scattered. Farzaneh is sitting in the middle of it all, naked, wearing her white porcelain mask. There is something alien about her, not just her nudity or the mask. I don't put it together until I see the smatterings of black locks all around her on the floor. It's her hair. She's cut off all her hair.

"What the hell? What have you done to yourself?"

"You'll leave. When you see me like this."

"Leave? What are you talking about?"

"It's for the best."

"Why have you done this?"

"So you can see me."

"Take off the mask."

"Just go."

"Take it off. Please."

There's a tremor in my chest as the word 'please' comes out, softness, a plea for contact. The sentiment breaks the despair in the room. She sits there in her impassive mask, looking up at me, contemplating, and then pulls it off her face. Her expression is fallen, defeated. Her hair is chopped into uneven clumps less than an inch long. I try to repress the thought but it occurs to me anyway: she looks more beautiful than ever.

"Finally," I say.

"Finally?"

"You're beginning to understand what we have."

"What makes you think that?"

"Because you couldn't betray me."

"It was horrible. My body was all knotted up."

"It was meaningful."

She pulls at a purple throw by her side and covers herself.

"I hope it's that," she says. "If it's that then everything is normal. I'm just a normal girl experiencing a normal loss of freedom."

I step to her side, sit down and pull her into my arms.

"I don't think you have any claim on being normal."

She laughs through her nose. A strain in her body loosens. Her head becomes limp on my chest. I stroke her scalp. My fingertips weave through the crevices in her jagged hair. We're together again. I can feel it.

"I need to tell you something," she says, "but you have to promise not to laugh. You have to take it seriously."

"Okay."

"I've never told anyone about this before."

"Okay. I promise."

"You have to swear."

"I swear."

"It's about the moon."

"The moon?"

She takes a breath.

"After my mum died, I felt as though a great weight was pushing down on me. Whenever I closed my eyes I felt like I was falling. It was a physical sensation. I would lie there in bed and suddenly scream or cry out, because I thought I was about to crash against the ground. Then, one night, after months of this, I had a dream. One of those vivid dreams that changes you somehow. You know the ones I mean?"

"Yes," I say, squeezing her hand. "I know."

"I was falling through the blackness, afraid, everything was chaos and fear, but then the moon appeared. Full and shining. Just by looking at it, everything became centred and still. I wasn't falling anymore."

"That sounds nice."

"I'm not finished."

"Sorry."

"The moon, it didn't speak exactly, but it let me know that there was a plan for me, that I wasn't alone. It told me that I was special, there was a path set out for me, that my life wouldn't be like everybody else's. I'd find something more... When I woke up, the crushing weight had lifted, but something wasn't right. It was the middle of the night. There was a cramp in my stomach. My crotch was moist. I put my hand down and realised that I was bleeding. I'd started my first period. I looked out between my curtains and there was a full moon. Somehow, I knew that it was the same moon that had spoken to me in my dream. I wasn't on my own. There was something out there, watching over me."

I stroke her neck.

"Did it feel like it was connected to your mum, the moon?"

"No. I knew she was gone. This was something else. Something deeper. It meant that the world wasn't meaningless, that everything still made sense."

"And you still believe it, that the moon spoke to you?"

"It was the only thing I ever believed. Right up until I was sixteen my period always started on the day of the full moon. I'd look out my bedroom window and there it would be, looking down. My protector. The months seemed so long back then. The rhythms of the cycles."

"So, what happened?"

She shifts in my arms and settles again.

"I started having sex. I went on the pill. My cycles came out of sync. I suppose I started thinking about other things. I still had the confidence the dream had given me, the lack of fear and grief, but I didn't feel connected to the moon anymore. When I looked up, it was just the ordinary moon. I lost that feeling of being in the right place, of everything being centred and inevitable."

"But something's changed?"

"Maybe it's being with you, feeling connected to something for the first time since my dad died, but I feel like I need to go back, find out what it was about. I don't want you to think I'm crazy for trying though."

I tense my arms around her and pull her close. I have the sensation that physical contact isn't enough, that no matter how near I bring her to my own body she will never be able to slip into the comfort of my care. I'll never be able to bring her a feeling of communion. It is a worry that I've never had before, a sad kind of love.

"I don't think you're crazy," I say. "I've had that feeling. That everything's exactly how it's supposed to be. Sometimes, when I'm skating, I get to the point where I feel like everything is balanced and true. Things couldn't be any other way. Especially since I've been with you. It's one of the best feelings there is. If you can have that in your life, I want you to have it."

"I felt like I couldn't talk about it, like if I said anything it would all come undone. But I think it's different with you. I don't need to be alone. I can tell you about it."

"If you think it was real, this connection you had, I'm not going to tell you it wasn't."

"I was just so used to it being a secret. Sometimes keeping things inside helps keep them real."

"And now?"

"I thought I had to lose you, to get it back, but I don't know. Maybe I don't. Maybe you can help me."

"I'm here for you. Whatever it takes."

"I'm so glad I found you."

"I can't imagine my life without you."

"We're going to make it, aren't we?"

"Definitely."

The weight of her body lolls onto me, then lifts again.

"What if this can never be what you want it be?" she asks.

"It can. It is."

"But what if it never gets any better?"

"I'm with you. That's all I want."

She starts kissing my neck and cheek, but with such desperate passion that I'm confused. As her lips reach mine, I try to hold her away but she doesn't let up. She pulls at my clothes. Her purple throw is lost in the commotion. She pushes herself onto me until my body responds. She grabs my penis and guides it into her, gouging away, her shoulders back, her face tilted upwards. She grinds up and down on me and touches herself until she releases a dark moan. Her pelvis judders and twitches. For the first time, as she comes, I don't feel connected to her. Nowhere near. Yet, she seems to have got off with more intensity than usual.

"Now you," she whispers.

"I'm okay," I say.

I pull her body down onto me and stop her motions. She resists for a second but then relaxes, satisfied that she is satisfied. Holding her close, the weight of her body on top of mine, mess and hair around us, there is a void in my chest. I'm distracted, emotionally disengaged. My love for her is somewhere, I can sense it, but it isn't in my mind or my limbs or my chest. Farzaneh's weight increases. She has fallen asleep. I look up at the ceiling. I can barely breathe.

TWO

The night before New Year's Eve, lying in Farzaneh's bed smoking a joint, I'm wondering why everything feels different. She's on her side with her back to me, writing in her notebook. Just a few weeks ago, the walls were more bustling than that first time I walked in here. Pages of writing covered pages of writing. There were paintings on top of drawings, clippings stuck on top of pictures. There were quotations, leaflets and postcards. And every creation, every string of words and use of colour, contained a memory, a moment of shared affirmation. The walls were the sum of our actions, the choices we had made to represent our shared existence. Then, in a fit of despair, because she couldn't bring herself to betray me, she tore it all down. Now, the walls are bare except for the stencilled impression of my body and the smears of paint on top of it from the first time we had sex.

"I miss the walls," I say.

Farzaneh's body becomes rigid and her notebook shuts halfway.

"Don't," she says.

I rest the joint in the ashtray, roll onto my side and move my stomach to her spine.

"Don't what?"

"I just think you should stop talking."

"Why?"

"You've been on the verge of this for weeks."

"I don't know what you're talking about."

Farzaneh sits up and puts her notebook down on the bedside table.

"You're going to ruin everything."

"Why would I ruin everything?"

"You can never just *be*."

"Be what?"

"Still. Motionless. Free. You claw at time. Try to punctuate it. Try to possess it. You need to put your hands all over something and own it. You can't just let things lie."

"Where is this coming from?"

"What we had is changing. The intensity is dwindling. It's becoming something else. You want to label us, before it's gone, so you can hold on to the story of what we are."

"All those things we made. The walls. I've never done anything like that before. Those three months…"

"We made some stuff. Now it's in a suitcase. Let's move on."

"Okay," I say, frowning. "I thought it meant something to you. It meant something to me."

She doesn't respond.

The next morning Farzaneh is sitting on the edge of the bed when I wake up, wearing a cold expression that I've never seen before. Her eyes are narrow and serpentine. Her mouth is tight and pursed, ready to strike.

"Do you realise that you've never spoken to me about being on the pill?" she says. "We've never used a condom. You realise that, don't you?"

My head is fuzzy from last night's weed. I'm confused by her seriousness.

"Of course. But you wouldn't have let me. I mean, I saw the packet in the bathroom and I just—"

"I'm not taking another pill. Never. I'm not filling my body with chemicals and hormones anymore. I won't do it. Not for you. Not for anyone."

"I never asked you to. I just thought you preferred it—"

"Do you really think that's the point? Look, just get out of here, would you? I don't want to be near you right now."

She stands up.

"Why are you doing this?" I ask.

"Do you think I was joking when I said I wanted to get my cycles back in sync with the moon? Do you think what I really meant was that you could just keep fucking me without protection?"

"What is this? If you want to change the contraception we use you just have to let me know. Say something. It's not like you've been pushing me away. This is about last night, isn't it?"

"It's got nothing to do with last night."

"Maybe I have been thinking about taking the next step, calling this what it is. What's so bad about trying to own what we've got, being proud of it?"

"This is about me and my body, not your male pride."

"Male pride?"

She turns her back to me.

"Nobody belongs to anybody. I don't belong to anybody."

I sigh.

"Maybe you're right. Maybe it is time we took a couple of days, had a bit of space."

"Space? Don't make me laugh. You don't know the meaning of the word."

"What's got into you?" I ask, climbing out of bed.

"All we do is hang out in this room, smoke weed, and fuck. You only ever leave to skate or study."

"So? What do you want to do?"

"I don't know. Something else. We're in London. I'm pretty sure there's something else to do out there."

"Okay. I'm going. I'll leave you to figure it out."

"Good."

I put my clothes on, walk into the bathroom and grab her packet of pills. On the way back through, I present them to her face and then throw them in the waste paper bin. She turns her head away with disdain.

I skate back to the morgue with my shoulders hunched and my hands in my pockets. The sky is low and white, the air cold and thin. There are letters in my box: student warden meetings I've missed, information about my loans, overdraft letters from the bank; things I've been ignoring. I go back to my room and toss them onto my desk. I'm not sure what to do with myself. I haven't spent any time alone for months. I end up pulling a shoebox full of old childhood memorabilia out from under my bed.

I flick through a couple of old notebooks: embarrassing confessions, banal ideas, my first attempts at writing philosophy. There's a photograph of a teenage girl I can't remember; pretty with a moody haircut. It takes a while for the story to come back. It's the girl I lost my virginity to. How could I forget her? I rummage deeper into the box, scanning old notes, reading old birthday cards, toying with random keepsakes. There's a tiny gold ring with a heart on it. Whose was that? A weird purple crystal. Everything looks alien, like it belongs to someone else. There's no meaning in any of it. I pack the stuff away and slide the box back under the bed.

I decide to scroll through the contacts in my phone. Abdul SK8? Annie P? Beck? They're just names. I can't recall their faces or who they are. It's a digital catalogue of no ones. My past doesn't belong to me. Only one name has any presence: *Farzaneh*. It lifts off the screen and turns my gut. I scroll down until another name arrests my attention: *Jake*. There's a memory, a face, a voice. He's part of London, part of not feeling alone in a big city. A friend. I tap to call him and put the phone to my ear.

"Come on, you slag!" he shouts, answering.

There's loud music and the hubbub of a large group of

people at his end. I rub my temples and smile. It's refreshing to hear his voice.

"Jake?"

"That's my line. Don't let that board duster near it. No, I can't, I'm on the phone."

"Jake? Can you hear me?"

"What's with the phone call? Have you been sent back to two thousand and one? Are you involved in some kind of space odyssey?"

"No. I just—"

"I presume you've been getting laid."

"What? Why?"

"Why else do you ever disappear off the face of the planet?"

"Sorry."

"So, what went wrong?"

"I don't know. It went weird."

"No, mate. This is weird, where I am. I can literally see a guy snorting coke off a bird's cleavage. The whole place has gone totally fucking *Robocop*."

A cheer rises around him. It turns the sound in my earpiece into distorted static. I move the phone away from my face and look out the window, down at the brown canal and bare willows.

"I just thought we could go for a quiet drink somewhere," I say. "Catch up."

"Quiet drink? It's New Year's fucking Eve."

"Yeah. I know. Forget it."

"Don't put yourself in the corner, Baby."

"I'm not. I'm fine. I'll just have a smoke or something."

"Oh God, I can hear the violins from here. Sit tight. I'll pop round. But we're going dancing."

"No, not dancing," I say, but he's already hung up.

I have a shower and change. Jake comes round an hour later. He's gurning, full of energy and agitating about in the corridor. His face looks bonier and older but his newfound gauntness hasn't dampened his spirit. His eyes are still eager and full of life.

"Got a right pharmacopeia in my bag," he says, shutting my door with an unintended slam, jigging around on the balls of his feet.

"Do you even know what a pharmacopeia is?"

"It's a shit load of drugs is what it is."

From nowhere, he produces two fingertips covered in MDMA and pushes them into my mouth. An acrid chemical taste explodes on my tongue and inner cheek. I rush to my sink and slurp at water, noticing that I'm not spitting the MDMA out but swallowing it down. Jake starts impersonating an astronaut on the moon, walking around aimlessly with slow, arching steps. I dry my hands and watch him with a smirk.

"We going to mix some tunes while we wait for you to come up then?"

He moonwalks over to my laptop, starts up a DJing programme and plays a medium-tempo techno track. As the high-end percussion joins the kick drum he starts tapping cocaine out of a baggie onto my desk.

"It's a bit early in the day for all this, isn't it?"

"People wait until it gets dark because they're ashamed," he says, chopping and swiping cocaine into two lines with a credit card, "because things can happen at night that can't happen in the day. Fuck that. It's New Year's Eve and I have no shame."

"Yes. Let's be shameless Mancunians. That's not a cliché at all."

He smiles and turns back to the laptop, searching for the next track. It's been a while since I've listened to electronic music. It sounds flat and soulless in my ears, like machines punching the clock a hundred and twenty times a minute. Jake's head is shifting from side to side as he makes a bad job of a mix. Beats trip over each other. Everything is out of time and chaotic. He gives up, hits the sync button, swipes the digital crossfader over, moves away from the laptop and dances in the middle of the floor. His spine and neck are jolting up and down in time to the beat. His arms are waggling around.

"This tune is fucking cerebral," he says. "Let's smash these lines."

We snort the cocaine and he carries on dancing. I sit down on the bed and start skinning up, sniffing through the chemical burn in my nostril. My heart beats fast and my cheeks radiate heat. Jake's limbs flit about in my peripherals. Three techno tracks pound by while I smoke the joint. Jake isn't interested in smoking any.

"Downers are for downers," he says.

"Since when?"

"Since Yola."

"Since YOLO?"

"Yola. Yo-la."

"I don't know what that is."

He shakes his head, switches the music over to dubstep and turns the volume up. The wobble of the bass shakes the plaster on the stud walls. At first, I'm grimacing because it sounds like someone's choking a computer game to death but during the second track the rhythm begins to creep into me. It starts making sense; the machines and the information; the paradox of seeking the tribal in the mechanised. I can hear it. My head is nodding and my legs are beginning to jig.

I stand up. It's particularly easy to stand up. My limbs and body are light. A beat is about to drop, the synthesisers are hitting their highest pitch, a crashing cymbal is echoing to the point of distortion, the tune is quoting Simon Reynolds with a reverberated, vocoded and double-delayed voice, "MDMA is the remedy, for the alienation, caused, by an atomised society," then bang, the beat and bass drop and I'm wiggling around the floor, catching the shapes of the sounds from the speakers and throwing them back at the universe.

Some part of me can see that Jake and I are dancing in my bedroom, high in the middle of the afternoon, and thinks it's a little bit strange, but most of me is thinking that everything is weightless, and I feel so good, and the music is great.

"See, we should go out and dance," says Jake, filling a glass with water at my sink. "We're dancing. The world is dancing. We should all be dancing together!"

"No," I say, smiling. "I can't. I'm too unhappy."

"Unhappy? Why?"

"Because I'm in love."

"Me too, mate," he says, laughing, wrapping his arms around me.

I laugh and hug him back.

We drink water and dance some more. I'm not sure when it happens or when he convinces me, there's quite a lot of cocaine and MDMA involved, but suddenly it's dark and we're walking down borderline-creepy streets full of old warehouses in Hackney Wick.

"Where are we going?"

"We're looking for a little birdy," says Jake, sniffing.

He's looking at the graffiti on the warehouse walls. I'm staring up at all the still cranes; luxury flat construction is on hold for the holidays.

"It's cold. Can we just go back?"

"Forwards. Always forwards."

We wander down an alley between two tall concrete walls, beside intruder-proof fences, through an abandoned carpark, past dead-looking buildings.

"Yes," he says.

He's looking at a little blackbird stencilled onto the corner of a warehouse. He turns down the side into an unlit ginnel. I follow him.

"Where are you taking us?" I whisper.

We get to an old iron door covered with graffiti. Jake turns on the screen of his phone and moves it around the surface until he finds another image of a little blackbird.

"This is it."

He swings the iron door open and the distant throb of a beat invites us in. The dark corridor is intermittently lit with glow sticks on the floor. We pass through the darkness, following the pink, blue and green florescent worms, and the bass of the beat becomes more and more present. At a black door, Jake turns to me with a smile. I see the skull beneath his skin.

"Let's get fucked up," he says.

He opens the door and techno kicks pound the air around us. A wave of heat sweeps out of the doorway and my cold body moves in towards the warmth. There are flashing lights, visualisation screens, lasers, towers of speakers, a makeshift bar made out of rusty barrels and long pieces of wood, and hundreds of people dancing.

"How does this exist?" I shout, over the music.

"Yola," Jake shouts back, tapping my shoulder, pointing over toward a group of eight people dancing in a tight circle near the back.

We walk over and the circle opens up. Arms fly into the air and smiles and cheers rise among them. Jake goes straight into the arms of a girl with the sides of her bleach-blonde head shaved. She looks deeply entrenched in the drugs and dancing scene; skimpy party clothes with a neo-hippy, eighties work-out edge and about twelve visible tattoos. She jumps in circles with Jake, both of them ecstatic. He then receives three or four hugs from some of the others and turns and gestures towards me. The smiles persist and they beckon me into their circle.

"This is Yola," says Jake, shouting into my ear.

Yola pushes her face forward towards me, opens her mouth wide and waves her hands around. Her loose vest hangs low and I see both of her pear-shaped breasts, braless, with large pink nipples, swinging from side to side. My eyes bulge and I try to smile back, forcing myself to look into her electric blue eyes.

People keep moving their mouths, looking at me, but I can't hear what anybody's saying. We dance together and stare into space when the beats lull. We smile at each other, dance again. Jake directs all his energy towards Yola. He can't take his eyes off her. She spends most of her time dancing with her eyes closed. Her jaw is protruding and her hair is wet with sweat. Occasionally, she opens her eyes and looks at Jake and they hug and rub their hands over each other. She loses herself in him but then passes back into the music, pulls away and starts dancing again.

At midnight, the music pauses for a half-ignored ten-second countdown. When the MC gets down to 'one' the speakers erupt and pump out a kaleidoscopic storm of electronic noise. The lasers and strobes swipe and flash in jagged paroxysms of light and darkness. The DJ jumps multiple tracks and samples back and forth, overlaps them, stops and starts them, juggles the chaos, and when he finally lets a four-four beat play everybody screams and whoops. There's laughing, shouting, hugging and jumping in circles. My brain is overwhelmed by the noise and commotion so I walk out of the crowd over to the wall.

I try to ring Farzaneh but the line won't connect. My eyes roll. I'm in a disgusting toilet with cocaine-burnt nostrils, somebody banging on the cubicle door. I wander back into the main room. Faces warp in the laser light. Nobody looks human, their features shift between amphibian and demonic. I stumble over to Jake. He puts three Rizla bombs full of who knows what into my hand. He has reptilian scales on his face. I sweat, swallow two of the bombs and jostle my spine to the music with my eyes closed. I have a plastic bottle of water in my hand that stays cold and full for hours, my hand aching with it, but the next bottle is warm and empty in seconds. A poorly-thought-through whiskey leaves my face sweating and my horizon seesawing. I lurch over to a corner and slouch down onto a cushion. I'm surrounded by strangers slumped like corpses.

"She's called Farzaneh," I tell them.

I inhale from a joint somebody passes to me and excited little ions spread out from my lungs into my bloodstream. It doesn't taste like weed, it tastes like sunlight bouncing on water. Each atom in my blood is positive and traceable. I'm following them all through my veins, around and around. I pass the joint along. Faces change and bodies move.

"She's called Farzaneh," I tell them.

The music blares on. This guy starts listening to me about Farzaneh. He keeps putting these tiny piles of white powder on the tip of his little finger, hovering them under my nose, and I keep sniffing and it keeps stinging, and it burns worse than coke or MDMA. All the time he's nodding and agreeing but I feel like I'm sinking away from him, down into a black swamp, and there's a deepening well above me.

"Where's my money?"

I look around in the darkness, straining to see the source of the words. The music is in slow motion; raw static and wobbles in space. I can feel hands in the blackness, inside my swamp. The dark mud is moving.

"Where's my money?"

"Get the fuck off him."

Black marsh moves around all over me.

"He owes me thirty quid. He took six hits."

I'm back on the floor watching Jake grab the shirt of the guy with the tiny piles of white powder. The swamp, the well; both are gone.

"You're a fucking pusher, mate, and you best move along. This is my girlfriend's party."

Jake shoves him into the crowd with two fists and then comes back over to me. My eyes roll. His hands touch my face, shake my skull, pat my cheeks.

"What are you doing over here with the ket-heads? I thought we were having a nice time. It's New Year. We're dancing."

"I told you I didn't want to dance," I mutter.

He doesn't hear me.

"Let's get a little bump in you. Lift you out of that K-hole."

"I don't want it. You think you can push a button in your head but you can't."

I pull away from him, roll onto my side and stumble up onto my feet.

"Hey. Come back. Where are you going?"

"I'm in love," I say.

The music isn't music. It's a cloud of magnetised iron filings, shadowy vibrations that slip between the gaps in my molecules. I'm mostly space, emptiness everywhere, and the air and the sound is erupting, exploding through me, knocking against my electrons and neurons. I make it to the exit and shut the door behind me. Everything becomes still. The atoms of my existence regroup.

Following fluorescent worms down the black corridor, the atmosphere is freezing and hollow, a stark vacuum without noise or heat. The walls are bending and my shoulders are jutting into hard surfaces that aren't there. People lurk against the edges in the shadows. I nearly trip over somebody's knee but it happens somewhere far away. I'm in a cable car, floating above mountains in the night sky, and the foot and the kneecap are on the floor, impossibly far away.

After struggling with the heavy iron door I'm out in the real world, ears throbbing and ringing, between two warehouses, the black sky above me. I notice a cigarette in my hand and, confused by its presence, take a drag. There's a flash of the girl who gave it to me. A pink cotton dreadlock. Was there really a slug on her face? My blood speeds up with the nicotine, its flow sharp and alive.

In an abandoned car park, pins and needles rise in my left arm. There's a cold sweat on my back. My neck is burning. I'm convinced that I'm about to have a heart attack. This is it. I'm going to be a tragic news story, a pitiful statistic: a student overdose in Hackney. The urge to stop and rest is immense but on some level I know if I pause I'll probably collapse and freeze to death in the street. A firework goes off somewhere. I hear a scream. The fences along the pavement look oppressive. Death sits in the shadows of a parked car with black windows.

I make it back to a road where things are happening. Faceless people wait outside kebab and chicken shops. Taxis pull up and spew out drunken limbs and stooping spines. Neon signs shine in the shapes of butchered meat. A black doorman with crocodile eyes stands outside an invisible club, beside an alleyway that a crackhead wouldn't walk down.

The bridge over the canal provides a moment of respite. I collapse my weight onto an ice-cold iron girder and stare out across the water. My eyes can focus in on anything that they want to: a leaf on a tree, a ripple on the water of the canal. I hear a couple having an argument. It sounds like they're right beside me.

"So what if it's New Year? All the more reason to break things off."

"Why do you keep doing this? Every time we go out?"

When I turn my head to see them I realise that they're at an inaudible distance; across the green, over by the road, a hundred metres further along than me. I turn to tell Jake about my new spider senses but he's not there. I panic, paranoid. How long have I been on my own? I hear a memory of myself talking to him less than five minutes old. Was I talking to myself? Is the memory even real? I take my weight off the bridge and time jumps off it.

Standing on my bed, gently bouncing up and down without my feet leaving the mattress, in time to the sound of a needle grinding and flicking on the eternal last loop of a record, I could be anywhere. I feel high up. I move my arms to the needle's secret melody and then I hear a giggle. I open my eyes and Farzaneh is in front of me, smiling. Then I realise that I don't even own a record player, she does, and that my eyes are still closed. I open my eyes again, the definite physicality of eyelid movement this time, and she's not there.

I step down off the bed and move over to my window. Looking out at the willows I see evil faces in the shades and shapes of the ropey branches hanging down into the canal. Is there something menacing in me? In the world? The dead eyes of the faces look like portals into another dimension. If I could jump through them I'd be nowhere.

I close my eyes and slip into geometric oblivion. A place where magic lines and hologram coloured shards weave and shape themselves together with majestic originality. *Where is she?* I wonder, sliding around in the variegated abyss, leaning against the windowsill. There is such complex symmetry, such vastness of shape and concept, but it all feels empty. She's not here.

THREE

It strikes me that I'm almost halfway through my course. After all those hours sitting in the same lecture halls, shuffling out into corridors and courtyards with our shoulders touching, day after day, the same faces, I'm still none the wiser about any of them. I'd probably feel worse about it if groups and cliques had formed but they all keep themselves to themselves. There are smatterings of pairs but they are awkward, muttering acquaintanceships, snarky, critical alliances. I had fantasies of meeting charming egotists who read Plato in Greek and Nietzsche in German. Scholars in a state of self-imposed predigital consciousness, smoking and drinking too much, taking drugs and indulging in primal sexual exploration. Instead, they all look tired and morbid, pale and weak. When my lectures finish I just want to get out of those stuffy rooms and go for a skate to clear my head. I sometimes borrow a book from somebody, or go for a coffee to talk about an essay, but really it's just Farzaneh, she's the only one I see.

Things have been getting better between us. Every week, we make sure we spend at least one night or day out of the house doing something new, and a night or day apart. We have sex using condoms. Everything is how she wanted it. Still, February's short, dark days seem to be making her irritable so, when I hear her drunken heels clonking and scraping on the pavement outside, moving towards the front of the house, I look around the room for signs of mess and general ineffectualness.

I'm in her bedroom after a shift at the restaurant, a sheen of grease on my face and the faint smell of stone-baked pizza bread in my hair. I've been wrapped up in the research for a Heidegger essay, my eyes tiring, but I'm anxious not to exasperate Farzaneh's bad mood. I brush some ash from the duvet cover and rush to put a couple of cups and glasses into the kitchen sink.

Downstairs, the front door slams. The windows up here vibrate and release a couple of shivery prangs. Feet pound up the stairs. I neaten up my notes and my books. Farzaneh storms in and swings the door back into its frame behind her. The crack and slam is followed by a flurry of objects being flung around. Her bag towards the desk, her earrings and bracelets onto the top of the chest of drawers.

"What's wrong?" I ask, struggling to shift from reflecting on presence and existence to being present and existing.

"My friends are idiots."

An acidic wine fog is permeating from her pores. She turns her back to me and rushes the fingertips on both hands around her scalp, undoing the manicured elfish look of her recently styled short hair.

"Idiots?"

"Clichés."

"I take it you didn't have a good time?"

She turns to face me.

"I'm never giving you another blow job in my life. Never."

"Okay," I say, trying not to sound amused.

Threads are snapping in her.

"It's demeaning. Disgusting. I won't do it."

"I've never asked you to."

"Don't be so pathetically compliant. Why do you pretend you're not a man?"

"What?"

"I know what you think about when you fuck me."

"What do I think about?"

"What all men think about."

"And what's that?"

She makes an exasperated nasal groan.

"I'd never want you to do anything you didn't want to do. You know that."

"So, you agree. It's demeaning. You've let me get down on my knees and demean myself."

"It's not like I don't go down on you. It's good. Generous. It doesn't have to be about power. What is this?"

"Tash and Riz just went on and on about sucking their boyfriend's cocks all night; how they do it, how often, what they do with their tongues. Jazz couldn't be bothered to show her face because she's too busy sucking off her new man, Sunila's still getting over sucking off her ex and Elle seems to define her identity by running through the lists of all the men she's ever sucked off. They're a disaster. I feel trapped when I'm with them. Gone. It's awful."

"Is Elle the one with the distended jaw?"

"What?"

"Nothing. Carry on."

She starts getting undressed and puts her long-sleeved pyjamas on; a sign that she doesn't want to have sex. I move my books and notes from the bed, strip to my boxer shorts and lie by the wall. I hear her washing her make-up off aggressively at the sink in the bathroom. She continues to complain through the doorway:

"Not a single woman I know understands what it is to be part of this world on their own terms. We graduate in four months. We're going out into the world. The real world. How they think, it's terrifying." She walks in from the bathroom and climbs into bed. "They don't know what the inner life of a woman should be like. Nobody's ever told them. Nobody wants them to know."

I nod and try to project sincerity but, sensing my secret

amusement at her drunken melodrama, Farzaneh turns away from me, curls up and tucks the duvet under her chin. I put my hand on her shoulder.

"Four months. Wow. Sometimes I forget you're a year older."

"That's not my point here."

"No. I know. They're monsters."

She turns her head and whips a curious but moody look at me, showing me that I'm not her enemy right now but that she's also not in the mood to play.

"Is there anything else going on?" I ask. "It's not like you to get so upset about your friends."

She sighs and turns her head back to me.

"My periods are still wrong," she says, sadder now. "I've missed it again."

"Is it the full moon already?"

"Yes."

"I'm sorry, honey. Maybe next time?"

She doesn't respond. I lie back and try to make my sigh inaudible.

In the morning, when I wake up, there is a wet throb in the centre of me. As the unconscious fog dwindles, I realise that Farzaneh is beneath the covers giving me a blow job.

"Hey, what are you doing? You don't have to do that."

She stops.

"You're right though. I should want to please you."

She sounds upset.

"Are you crying?"

"A little bit."

She puts her mouth around my penis again.

"Stop. Stop."

She lifts her head.

"No. It's okay. I want to."

It's back in her mouth. I reach down and pull her head up.

"But I don't want you to. Not when you're like this."

She wraps her arms around my torso, pushes her head onto my stomach and starts sobbing.

"Why does everything I do make me feel like a freak?"

"I don't want you doing something you don't like doing."

"Nobody likes it. They just do it. Because not everything has to mean something."

She starts wriggling down towards my crotch again. I grab her by the armpits and pull her back up towards me.

"Let's go out for breakfast," I say. "Read our books."

She lies limp on my chest.

"That sounds nice."

"Nicer than sucking a dick?"

She laughs and sniffs and wipes her eye with the back of her hand.

"Shut up."

I hold on to her.

She's quiet for a few minutes, easing her way back to me. There's an authenticity in how she's holding me, a trust. Her seesawing between being present and absent in our relationship has been constant since New Year but when she's vulnerable like this, close to me, I forget all the distance. I'm with her. All the nonsense and tension leaves and sensations of love and commitment well up in me. I feel so glad to have her in my life, so happy to be holding her.

"I'm sorry I'm such hard work," she says.

"You're not."

"I am. It's okay. I know I am. Why do you put up with me?"

"I just do. I always will."

"It's funny, but I actually believe you. I know you will."

"I will."

"Maybe I don't need the moon. Maybe I just need you."

"I'd like that," I say.

FOUR

We walk down a street in Hackney Wick lined with warehouses and factories that have all been converted into open-plan one-bedroom flats and studios. Almost every long window with a light on reveals a high ceiling, white walls, a mezzanine bed and a tasteful art print or film poster. Tonight is part of our ongoing pursuit of London, and not staying locked away in Farzaneh's bedroom. Last week I took us to see a piece of theatre loosely based on a Thomas Pynchon novel upstairs in a pub near Angel. This week Farzaneh has found out about a punk gig she wants to go to. There is a growing sense that we are a couple looking for something pleasing in the world, but that the world is displeasing, and we are displeased, and this feeling is normal, so maybe we'll be okay.

"Are you scared about graduating?" I ask.

The sky is midnight blue and it feels like a treat that it's not completely dark. The days are getting longer again.

"Not scared. Underwhelmed. In some ways, I feel like continuing to exist after university makes you complicit in an evil plot to destroy the world."

I smile.

"You could keep on studying. Do a Master's. You can afford it."

"I spent the last three months writing about the *Fateful*

Environment of Thomas Hardy's Wessex and I didn't learn a single thing that I didn't already know when I started. I'm not cut out for academia. I don't like spending my time trying to prove that my thoughts are arguments. They're not. It doesn't seem like the right way to relate to myself, or to other people's creations."

"Yes, that stance could be a bit of a problem if you did an MA."

"You know, these places are two grand a month."

"They look nice."

"Studios and one beds. Artists used to live down here, before they got priced out. People can't live alone in London anymore, or work part-time. When are artists supposed to make art?"

"I don't know."

"A city needs artists."

The street becomes more destitute further along. It's not clear whether the buildings have been converted or not. There are half as many street lights. The pavement and the road are buckled and full of dents and potholes.

"I think it's this one," says Farzaneh, stopping before a shadowy entranceway into a small, rundown warehouse.

"Who are these guys?"

"Just some band, I told you."

She presses a chipped silver button on a buzzer system. To the left of the button there's a strip of masking tape that has the words *Millennial Discord* scrawled onto it in black felt-tip pen.

"And it's a gig?"

The door makes a whirring sound and a mechanism clicks. Farzaneh pushes it open.

"Sort of. They live here. I think gigging costs too much these days, ferrying kit around in vans and taxis, promoters taking most of the door money, so they just invite people over, play music, sell merchandise."

We walk down a half-lit corridor covered in black-and-white

punk-style band posters. The dampened noise of fast drums and guitar fuzz pulses from somewhere up in front of us.

"And how did you find out about them?"

"A girl on my course. She said they were really *punk rock*, as though that was the best compliment on earth."

We get to a door with *Millennial Discord* spray-painted across it. The words breach the doorframe and move onto the walls on either side. Fast, violent band noise eats through the wooden door, the kick drum pounding against it from the other side, making it rattle and throb.

"So, what are we walking into here? A bunch of skinheads head-butting each other? A couple of stoners sitting in front of a band on the floor?"

"Open the door and find out."

I push the door open and music floods out with eardrum-piercing force, but as quickly as the sound spears out it stops. The song has finished.

We step into the room.

We're at the back of a crowd of about fifty people who are all standing and engaged with the band, cheering and shouting for the previous song while the amps release their final twinges and shrieks. None of the crowd notice our entrance. We slip in behind them, close the door and give a morbid-looking woman at a small table collecting 'donations' a couple of pounds each. She scribbles an *x* on our hands in permanent marker and points over to a rusty keg, implying that paying gives us the right to a drink. We take her up on the offer and move to the back of the crowd with two pints of weak lager in plastic cups.

It's a decent room for a small gig but it's impossible to see how the four band members at the back could all live here. Four bare mattresses are pushed up against the side walls, rags of clothes hung over them. There's a mezzanine jutting out on the far wall about eight feet high cluttered with broken amplifiers and instruments, and black bin bags which could be full of rubbish or quickly gathered and displaced possessions. Beneath the mezzanine, the band, three men and a woman, all in their mid- to late twenties, all sweating and agitated, are waiting for a lull. They seem to be infatuated with Sid Vicious: black leather, ripped T-shirts, ripped jeans, silver things twinkling all over them. The crowd is a mixture of punks, students, poor graduates and fashionable young professionals.

Farzaneh squeezes my palm with amusement and anticipation. The singer starts shouting with an aggressive, scowling voice:

> *"Generation rent. Generation debt. Generation*
> *Y-fucking-bother. Welcome to our shithole. We are*
> *Millennial Discord. One-two-three-four..."*

They burst into a couple of short, fast songs with intense, melodic choruses and tortured, screaming vocals. The seemingly simple lyrics and guitar work are actually complex and carefully considered. Their music is punk as art, and art as a noise pastiche, and they're good at it. Nothing sounds too simple or too overworked. It has as much appeal for eclectic musos as it does for people who just want to shake their heads and bang into each other. The choruses are particularly catchy:

> *"Burn the system.*
> *Burn the system.*
> *It doesn't work for me.*
> *I don't need it anymore."*

> *"We got nothing.*
> *Being left behind.*
> *We want nothing.*
> *Being left behind, left behind."*

"They're all right," I say to Farzaneh, over a white-noise finale while the vocalist screams *"left behind"* again and again.

After some woops and clapping, the wrought singer starts shouting into the crowd again.

"Nobody is born a punk. It's a choice you make. Because you don't like the way the world looks. So, you don't want the world to like the way you look. You want to get in its prissy little face. You want to say… one-two-three-four…"

"Hey, fuck you.
Fuck you too.
Hey, fuck you.
Don't give a fuck about you."

The hook of the song is immediately engaging. It's a perfect Ramones knock-off. The crowd starts bouncing at sharp angles, twice as pronounced as with the earlier tracks. Plastic cups half full of beer are being thrown over everybody's heads, Farzaneh's among them. She grabs me by the arm, forcing me to spill my own beer onto the floor, and pulls me further in. Elbows, knees and torsos jar into my sides and chest. At first, I feel jostled but then my limbs and joints begin to get swept up into it, banging into other people's hips and backs and arms. The violence of the crowd is nulled by my acceptance of it. There is no aggressive pointedness to any of the movement. The aim is disorder, and we all feel close to it.

The *fuck you* track descends into a twelve-minute throb of lead and bass guitar distortion and heavy drumming, the singer occasionally screaming *"fuck you"* with his teeth on the mic. The noise goes on and on, repeating the same patterns, edging closer and closer to turmoil but then grounding itself back in the hook, humming and pounding. It creates a tribal response in the crowd. We're lost in its chaotic rallying, knocking off each other's skin and bones, senses obliterated by the volume and the recurrence of the sounds.

When the band starts smashing their instruments against each other's, stamping on them and throwing them around, and the music begins to break away into destruction and uncalibrated noise, we all find ourselves surfacing from a dream we might have had about belonging to something, about touching something bigger than ourselves. There is a moment of quiet where our ears throb and we're not quite sure where we are, and then we all start cheering.

"Fuck you!" the singer shouts, without the aid of his now discarded microphone. "Buy a T-shirt or a record or get the fuck out of my landlord's flat!"

People laugh and clap and whistle and call out. A few dribs and drabs move towards the front to buy something but most people start huddling back towards the door. I stand still, moved by the intensity of the last ten minutes. Farzaneh pulls at my hand. I follow her back out through the warehouse and onto the street.

"I have to admit, they got under my skin," I say.

"It's a shame it's got to exist in a vacuum," she replies, "that London has forced them into a space where they don't matter, where they can't reach anyone."

"Isn't that the point though? It's a call to arms. Against the city. Against the culture. Besides, they reached *us*."

We're back on the well-lit portion of the street where all the warehouse flats look nice.

"I really connected with that last song," she admits. "I feel like it unlocked something in me."

"Me too. It was more real than anything I've seen or heard in ages."

"That whole aesthetic though. The way they live. The poverty. The graffiti. I mean, graffiti? The idea that graffiti could be outsider, or destructive, to this city, this megalithic monster… It barely even paints its toenails."

"It's an image, an attitude."

"That's the problem. It's not like they're down in Canary Warf with sledgehammers. 'I got a bad deal, it makes me angry, it's not fair, poor me.' That's the real message. It's got nothing to do with collective action. It's just about the self, and hurt vanity. But instead of telling you that, they're selling you the idea of rebellion, and revolution. It's bullshit."

"I can see that. But there's a difference between an artist and an activist, isn't there?"

"There's also a difference between an artist and a capitalist. They've moved their music from public spaces to private spaces, made a brand and products, and they live by promoting and selling those products. They're basically a corporation."

"I remember when you used to argue that it was good to subvert the system by playing its game, bringing the outside in."

"Life isn't a game though, is it?" she says.

"I thought it was convincing. Really angry. Really about now."

She turns to me with what seems like genuine worry.

"No," she says, "it was deceitful. Four people can't live in a one-bedroom flat, in filth, just so they can say they're free."

"But the gig was great. It doesn't have to change anything. It's a performance. It expresses an idea."

"Sometimes music induces something special. Like that last song, when they were playing that loop over and over again. It's like it conjures up the world behind this one. You can see it somehow. And when it happens, when you're in that world, it's so easy to find the deepest and most meaningful parts of yourself. It connects you to real things."

"Real things?" I ask.

"I can't just say that was great and I got something out of it and now it's over. It's not like that for me. That feeling triggers something. Helps me remember where I'm supposed to be."

We're about to step back out onto the main road where the bus routes run. I stop and face Farzaneh and take hold of both of her hands.

"But, it doesn't have to get you down," I say. "Or take you away from me. It's just a feeling. It's transient. You don't have to feel it all the time."

Farzaneh frowns and slips her hands out of mine, bringing one up to her stomach. There is a soft pain in her eyes.

"What is it?" I ask.

"It unlocked something…"

She wanders away from me, looking up into the sky, walking diagonally into the road. A car slows as she crosses in front of it and then carries on, the driver shaking his head.

"Farzaneh, careful."

She stops on a traffic island, looking up, pivoting around. A red double-decker bus passes on the other side of her, its driver pre-emptively pipping the horn due to the distraction in her motions. I run to her side.

"What are you doing?"

"I just came on."

She's still looking up at the sky but her eyes are now fixed on one spot. I look in the same direction. There's a vague circular glow loitering behind some moving clouds.

"Is that…"

"The moon," she says, resting her hand on her womb. "It's full. I can feel it."

"That's great but I think we should get out of the middle of the road."

"Wait."

The clouds break. As Farzaneh thought, the moon is bright and full. For a moment, standing by her side, looking up, some portion of its power slips into me and I perceive more than a meaningless circle of rock reflecting light in the sky. Farzaneh seems to think of it as a companion or a guiding light but, for me, looking at the moon reveals how insignificant and small I am. It releases me from the world and myself, helping me to momentarily disperse into the vastness of space. It's the same sensation as looking at the horizon or seeing the view from a mountaintop. A sense of gratitude prevails, directed outwards, towards the vague idea of beauty or being alive. I suppose, for Farzaneh, the moon is the sole provider of this release from the self, giving her access to something that she can't otherwise reach.

"I have to be alone," she says, pulling away from me, almost stepping out in front of a car.

The driver beeps. I pull her back and then walk her over to the pavement.

"No," I say. "That's not how this goes. Remember?"

"It is. I think it wants me to be on my own."

"What? No. It doesn't. You need somebody with you, so you don't walk into the road and end it all before it's begun."

"I'm sorry," she says. "It was always the same."

"I can help you with this. You know I can."

"You won't understand."

"I will. Look, I've been waiting for the right time but, I think I should just say it now."

"What?"

She looks down from the sky and into my eyes.

"We should move in together. At the end of this semester. Live together."

"What?"

"Since I met you, all I've wanted is to be with you. I've got to find a place anyway, and I want to live with you."

"But, I need time alone," she says, looking up at the sky again. "And I like my place."

"Just think about it. Think about how this came about. Your cycles are back on track. It happened when you were with me."

"Since I met you, I've felt like maybe there's a life I didn't know about."

"Me too."

"With me?"

"Yes."

"I'm not sure we're talking about the same thing."

"Will you give us a chance?"

She stares up at the moon, as though straining to hear it.

"Maybe," she says, holding her hand to her stomach. "Yes."

FIVE

We find a one-bedroom basement flat near London Fields. It's on a terraced street lined with large ash trees that have been cut down to leafless stubs. Each three-storey townhouse has a bay window; half of them destitute and ageing, the rest renovated and freshly painted. The window above our basement is tastefully rundown by a landlord who obviously cares about their property, but not too much. The flat has either been recently converted or spruced up after a period without tenants. It has freshly whitewashed living room walls, aquamarine tiles with bright white grout in the bathroom, a newly fitted kitchen and cheap but functional modern furnishings. Being the basement, we also get the access to the small back garden.

The disparity between our neighbours seems typical for this part of Hackney. There are house-rich poor people who have lived on the street for over thirty years, working class people who bought their first house here over twenty years ago, middle-class people who moved here within the last ten years and a silent majority of young and aging renters. There are also two small chunks of social housing, each with six flats, built into the hollows of houses that were destroyed by bombs in the blitz.

London housing hadn't sparked my interest in any significant way while I lived in student accommodation. I knew that rents were unreasonably high but my rent and bills just came straight out of my student loan payments at the start of each semester. Housing seemed connected to a culture of studying. Now it feels like I'm really here, living in the city, because I'm contracted to pay seven hundred and fifty pounds a month for half of a one bedroom flat – before bills. The hardship this will bring contains the thrill of a challenge. There are people on this street who live in basements and also own expensive German cars. If I want to stay here, I will need a full-time job in place before I graduate. There is zero leeway.

Moving in with Farzaneh should have been exciting. It should have given me a sense of union and joy. Instead, she has been distracted and irritable. The day we moved in, she broke down in tears while I was carrying a box into the bedroom with a head full of hopes. She wouldn't tell me what was wrong. I consoled myself with the idea that moving house was stressful.

"I don't think I want them to come," says Farzaneh.

"We can't back out. They're due any minute."

"It seems phoney."

"We're just having a couple of friends over. It doesn't have to mean we're middle-class sell-outs, or whatever it is that's bothering you. It's just some friends hanging out in a garden."

"I don't see why we couldn't just go to the park."

"Because we've got a new place and we want to have a drink and break some bread. Can you try to be just a little bit positive?"

"I don't even know them."

"You know Jake."

"Do I?"

"You'll get to know them."

"I feel like you're trying to make this into something I don't want it to be."

There are knocks on the front door, Jake's familiar silly knock with a few extra excited knuckles pattering around from Yola. All summer, they have been posting photographs of themselves that look like the advertising campaign for an explicit television show about sexy, wayward youth culture.

"Sorry, but it's too late. It's happening."

At the door Jake steps forward and we half shake hands, half hug on the doorstep. His clothing is more loose and colourful than it used to be: a paisley shirt, khaki shorts and a fishing hat. He looks easy-going and relaxed. Twenty-first century *Madchester*.

"Hey, buddy."

"Hey."

Farzaneh and Yola stand at an amicable distance, exchanging glances over our shoulders. Yola is wearing a white crop top with no bra, black hot pants and high-top trainers. She bounces towards me as soon as the hug with Jake breaks off and wraps her arms around me, planting her breasts on my chest in a haphazard, flesh is flesh, nothing is sexual fashion.

"It's been way too long," she says, pulling her head back but holding her arms around my waist, keeping our pelvises locked together.

Farzaneh glances over at us, hugging Jake with less committed contact.

"I know," I say, taking a step back. "Ages."

Farzaneh and Yola smile and acknowledge each other, hesitating over whether to make physical contact. Farzaneh places the tips of her fingers on Yola's tattooed upper arm, tilting her head. Yola mirrors this, placing her hand on Farzaneh's waist.

"Yola?"

Yola beams and smiles, feigning instant intimacy by scrunching up her nose.

"The one and only," she says, giving up on maintaining her distance, pulling Farzaneh towards her and giving her the same full body hug that she just gave to me, pulling her head back with their pelvises conjoined. "You're gorgeous, by the way. Just gorgeous."

We sit on the lawn in the back-garden and drink gin and tonics and pale ales, smoking cigarettes and joints. I've put out a sourdough loaf from the local bakery and plates of various cheeses, thinly sliced Italian hams and salamis, bowls of olives, and crisps and dips. They chuckle about the spread. Yola calls it 'fancy' in a silly voice and this dispels the last of my tension over Farzaneh's middle-class reservations. We pick at the food but focus more on the drinking.

An out and out transformation has occurred in Jake. His sharp, chauvinistic humour has given way to a more absurdist and ironic merriment. With Yola in his life, all his intellectual and sensual whims are being met, so he finds everything amusing. I prefer him this way. He seems content, and more himself.

Yola is constantly on stage, talking to the fifty people around you that you didn't know were there. By her third drink, she only stops talking to put slices of Parma ham into her mouth, and then talks through chewing them, wiping her greasy fingers on her tattooed thighs. She broadcasts the high points of her active social life, which is mainly based around organising illegal raves and parties but also modelling for subversive photographers and small-time fashion houses. She spends five minutes showing me semi-pornographic pictures of herself on her phone. I catch Farzaneh slipping her a loathing glance as she scrolls to a particularly audacious picture in which she's nude and covered in fake blood and says, "Oops, vagi-arna in that one." Jake laughs.

The more drunk Yola gets the more she assumes the centre. It becomes the getting to know Yola afternoon and, seeing no resistant forces, she revels in it for well over an hour before leaning back on her elbows and raising her face to the sun, deciding to ask us some questions of her own.

"You guys must be so committed," she says, folding a

piece of salami into her mouth and then wiping her fingertips on the back of her neck. "How long have you been together?"

"Maybe a year?" I say, looking at Farzaneh. "But we were hanging out for a while before that."

Farzaneh shrugs.

"Probably a year."

"Wow, that's fast. Moving in together. You must really know."

"Know what?" asks Farzaneh.

"That you want to be together."

"It felt like the right thing to do," I say. "We were spending all our time together anyway. And, this way, we don't have to live in two horrible shared houses with loads of random strangers."

"I like my horrible shared house, thank you very much," says Jake.

"I like home to be private," I reply.

"My place is a total wreck but I love it," says Yola. "We throw parties, meet lots of people. It can be a bit much, when it's eight in the morning on a Sunday and the techno's still pounding through the walls, but it's definitely where I need to be. It's London, you know? You can hide away in the suburbs when you're all dried up and ancient."

She laughs at the idea of being dried up and ancient, loud and cackling.

"There's no way I could live in a party house," I say. "I need quiet. I spend most of my time reading."

"You're a softie," she says, laughing, tugging my arm. "But you'd be surprised how quickly you adjust. You get into the spirit of it."

"How do you get any work done?"

She laughs, still holding my wrist.

"That's true. I hardly get any work done. But I'm scraping by."

"And what do you do at uni?"

"Occupational therapy. It can be a drag but I think it's

something worth doing. I've got my first placement in September so I'm going to have to tone down the partying, a lot. How about you?"

"Philosophy."

"I thought philosophy died, like, a thousand years ago," she says, smiling.

"Not for everyone."

"I mean, no offence, but didn't science bury all the old stuff like that?"

"Science can't tell you how to live your life, or how to think."

"Cool. So, you're really into it then. Do you want to be a philosopher? I mean, is that even a thing?"

"I used to want to write my own stuff but it's not really like that. It's mostly juggling other people's semantics."

Yola releases my wrist and puts her hand on my thigh.

"So, how do you do it? I mean, someone has to do it. How do you become a philosopher?"

"I don't know. I'm not sure you can, unless you're French. I guess you just have to write a book. Maybe do it as part of a PhD. See how it lands when you try to get it published."

"A book. Wow. I could never write a book. I couldn't sit still for long enough."

"I'm not sure I could."

"What's the alternative? What does your average Philosophy graduate do?"

"I have no idea. I didn't really think life through very well, did I?"

"You're great," she says, rubbing her hand up and down on my thigh, her greasy fingers leaving a light sheen. "Jake, I love this guy. He's so dry. How about you, Farzaneh? Didn't you just graduate? What's your plan?"

She pulls her hand away from my leg and focuses all her attention on Farzaneh, shoulders turned towards her.

"I don't like plans."

"No? What do you like?"

"I don't know. Poetry, maybe."

"Poetry? Ha! You two are perfect for each other. I mean, does poetry even *exist* anymore?"

"Yes," says Farzaneh, "it *exists*."

"Do people do it though? Can they survive off it, I mean?"

"It depends what you mean by survive."

"I mean, can poets pay their way by writing poetry?"

"Unsurprising."

"What is?"

"A handful of people survive off it. So, no. Not really. It doesn't attract consumers because it's not trying to sell you something. Which also means it can be honest, and fearless."

"But, what are you going to do for, like, a job? I mean, the rent in this town is fucking bananas."

"I don't intend to worry about that."

"That sounds practical," says Yola, amused.

"I don't really care what it sounds like."

"Hey, I didn't mean anything by it. I'm just joking around."

"Yes," says Farzaneh. "Why be serious about anything when you can be ironic about everything?"

Yola's face straightens. She's not threatened by Farzaneh. She's trying to be respectful by toning herself down but there's still joy in her eyes.

"Yeah, reject it all. Fucking anarchy, man. Why not?"

"You think I'm joking?"

"No. I think your parents must be rich."

"My parents are dead."

"Shit, sorry, I didn't mean to—"

"No. You're right. I have some money. I can afford to keep myself afloat. For a few years, at least."

"No, but—"

"Really. I hate pity."

Yola looks at Jake. He awkwardly bulges his eyes to imply that he didn't know about her parents and reaches over for her hand.

"But the world comes knocking," I say. "It's not like

you've inherited a hedge fund. It's a finite amount. You'll have to find a place in the world eventually."

"I have a place in the world."

"I'm not saying you don't."

"Each body is its own country," she says. "It has its own laws."

"But when you look at the bigger picture…" says Jake.

"I'm not interested in the bigger picture. I want to live in my own picture, in my own way, here, and now."

"I get it," says Yola. "That's why we party. You create the world you want to see around you."

"No," says Farzaneh. "That's just ignorance. And a false sense of entitlement. I'm searching for something deeper."

Yola's jaw drops in a mock outrage that is quickly losing its goodwill.

"How is it ignorance?" she asks.

"Just leave it," says Jake.

"No. I want to know. How is it ignorance?"

"Drugging yourself into euphoria, not acknowledging the pain and suffering in your world?"

"Parties are about bringing people together," says Jake, trying to divert the tension that is building between them. "That's what Yola gives people."

"Parties didn't work the first time," says Farzaneh, "they didn't work the second time, and they're certainly not going to work the third time."

"What are you talking about?" he asks.

"The hippies. The ravers. All they ever did was turn their backs on society, pursue their own childish ideations and let the neo-liberals have a field day. It was juvenile. Self-indulgent. That's not what I want for myself. That's not what I'm trying to achieve."

"There's a difference between the hippies and us," says Yola, "even between the ravers and us."

"Enlighten me."

"The hippies, the ravers, they were children, teenagers, left unequipped, and ignored. They were trying to create a new world, because their world had forgotten about them. Just by existing, by creating those communities, society had to look at them, it had to admit that they were there. It had to look around and ask itself how this had happened, how everything had become so atomised."

"That's true," says Jake. "That's so true. You should listen to her. She knows so much about this kind of stuff."

"But today's partiers are older," continues Yola, "and more secretive. They don't want the world to see them. They have jobs they can't afford to lose. They're informed, and political, but apathetic, in a state of arrested development. Unable to leave society, unable to join it. In debt, struggling to make rent, too poor to start families. Parties are where they shrug off the hopelessness of it all. Once a week, once a month, whatever fits, whatever they can afford, mentally, financially. Just to sense that they haven't been completely abandoned. There's a place for them, to feel good, or to feel nothing, to find themselves, or lose themselves, experience the true nature of their irrelevance."

"And I suppose that makes you their saviour," says Farzaneh, "the harbinger of their truth."

"I just help organise the parties, love. I'm on the dancefloor with the rest of them."

"It sounds like these people are in the habit of pitying themselves," says Farzaneh. "They're jealous of their parents' wealth, but they aren't poor. They have roofs over their heads, sanitation, electricity, food. So what if they can't afford property, or a room for each child? They need saving from their own cultural narcissism, not have it indulged with parties."

Jake laughs. Yola puts her hand on his thigh and squeezes.

"You think so?" he says.

"Yes. They need to grow up. Start facing their lives. Society doesn't owe them anything. If they feel like it's tricked them, or stolen from them, then more fool them. They should have followed their own rules. Made their own paths."

"That's not really how it works," I say.

"It is how it works," says Farzaneh. "It's exactly how it works. You have to see what's in front of you. You have to see how it really is."

"And that's what you're doing?" says Yola, smirking.

"Yes. I'm finding my own truth."

"Sure," says Yola. "With your inheritance."

"Her poetry is great," I say, jumping to her defence, desperately trying to change the tone of the conversation.

Farzaneh looks down at her hand which is ripping up grass.

"Yeah, the poetry," says Yola, with enthusiasm. "Some people have to make it, right? I love poetry."

"It's not about the fucking poetry," says Farzaneh. "I don't want to *make it*. I know it must be hard for you to understand but I don't write for that kind of vainglorious reason."

"*Okay*," says Yola, feigning amusement but angry now. "What are you going to do then?"

"I don't have to *do* anything."

"Why don't you? What? Do you think you're too unique for a day job?"

"Ease off," I say to Yola, making Jake's neck lengthen. "What if she is? Some people are."

"I'm not afraid of being demonised for thinking highly of myself," says Farzaneh. "You think you're a big deal too, don't you, but you're too weak-minded to admit it. You need it to come from someone else. You hide behind your screens and your tattoos, making yourself look tough and fearless, trying to police people into thinking you're some kind of free bird, but you're starved and empty."

"Hey. There's no need for that," says Jake, interjecting with an awkward and baffled laugh.

"So, you want to get real, do you?" says Yola. "You've got the emotional intelligence of a flea. You think you're the centre of the universe. You're the special one. You're the exception. Everything can be different for you."

"It's not my fault you can't see it in me, or that you're not brave enough to see it in yourself."

"You're just a narcissist, darling. There's nothing special about that."

"Let's dial this down a notch," I say.

"You're the one who describes your body to strangers as, let me get this right, a living piece of art. You're the one with two hundred pictures of yourself on your phone."

"Come on then," says Jake. "What is it, Farzaneh? What's so special about you?"

"I want you to leave," she says. "I'd like your condescending, narrow little minds to get the fuck out of our garden."

"Fuck this noise," says Yola, standing up.

"I think she's right," I say, looking at my wrist as though I'm wearing a watch. "It's time we called it a day here."

Jake stands up by Yola's side, then I stand facing them. Farzaneh stays sitting, staring straight ahead in a fury.

"You're a piece of work, love," says Yola, looking down at her, shaking her head. She turns to me and gives me a short hug, tapping our necks and collars together. "Good luck with her."

She struts out of the garden and into the kitchen.

"Right, I guess we're off then," says Jake.

"Graduation is a weird time," I say.

He looks at Farzaneh and nods.

"See you then."

He follows Yola into the kitchen and leaves. I wait until I hear the front door close. Yola's laugh, hysterical and unbound, arcs over the house and into the back garden, fading as they make their way down the street.

"Why did you do that?" I ask, sitting back down on the grass with Farzaneh. "Jake's my best friend. I know Yola's a bit much but you could have just bit your tongue."

"I bit my tongue all afternoon. She was insufferable. I couldn't stand seeing the bottom of her tits hanging out of that top for another second."

"Her tits? Are you serious?"

"She was disgusting."

"She's brash, but you didn't need to try and take her down like that."

"She was practically holding your dick all day."

"What? Is that what this is? I don't know if you noticed but I was supporting you the whole time. Were you jealous?"

Farzaneh takes a breath.

"No. Sorry. I think I'm just trying to manipulate you."

"Okay. So, what then?"

"I just hated her. Isn't that enough?"

"Is it because she was calling you out on the outsider stuff? I mean, even I'm a bit worried about what you're going to do."

"I've never met anybody so shallow."

"She's training to be an occupational therapist."

"Watching the way she shoved that meat into her mouth, everything was just taste buds, nerve endings, screens, skin, photographs, tattoos. Layers colliding. She was all surface. This world, as it is now, she belongs here."

"I didn't think she was that bad."

"I'm not saying she wasn't *fun*. I'm not a prude. I don't care how people dress, what they do, how they express themselves. Just, something about her made me realise…"

"What?"

"I can't eat meat anymore."

"Meat?"

"I don't want to consume anything with a mind."

"That's what you took from today?"

"The thoughtlessness of it. Devouring consciousness. As though you're entitled to it. As if it's just a surface detail. Did you see her, taking pictures of it?"

"The meat?"

"Yes."

"No. I didn't notice."

"I can't quite… I haven't put it into words yet. It just came to me. A voice."

"So, you're a vegetarian?"

Farzaneh grabs my leg.

"I think it might have been the moon," she says, a spark in her eyes.

"That told you to stop eating meat?"

She nods, and then a rare note of shyness engulfs her.

"Let's meditate tonight," she says, looking down. "Together."

"Meditate?" I ask, ignoring the sense of the irrational all around me, willing it away. "Sure. We can do that."

I stand up and start clearing the plates and glasses from the garden. When I'm done, Farzaneh is sitting on the lawn with her legs crossed and her eyes closed. I roll a joint and sit on the back doorstep smoking, welcoming the fuzzy lack of thought. The garden retains Yola's presence, an echo of her laughter, a sense of her careless and fun energy slowly dwindling down to nothing. Barbecue smoke drifts over the fence, the smell of charred animal flesh and burning coals. The airborne carbon deepens the amber hue of the dipping sun. Trains rustle and whir in the distance. A pink sizzle rises on the inside of my thighs from sitting on the grass in shorts without sun cream.

I roll another joint, determined to outlast Farzaneh's meditative period, since we've agreed to meditate together, but she goes on and on, not shifting or stirring. I don't know how long I've been staring into space. I'm stoned, with a bit of a headache from the early afternoon drinking. The birds are quiet and the blue night is beginning to darken. I missed whatever she said. She's sitting in the same spot, naked now. I didn't see her undress. I flick my eyes across all the visible windows, the number of our neighbours who could potentially see her. Fifteen? Twenty? Is it right to feel protective? Is her body just for my eyes? It's easy enough to make some neighbourhood creep start obsessing, turn him into something dangerous. Is that even what I'm worried about?

"Sorry. Did you ask me something?"

"It's got to be undone," she says.

"What does?"

"The flesh."

"You mean the meat?"

"I don't want it anymore."

"Okay," I say. "No meat."

She opens her eyes and turns her head my way.

"I thought you were going to join me?"

"You didn't ask."

"Come over."

I stand up and wait for a blood rush in my head to settle. The garden comes back into focus. I sit opposite her, less than a yard between us. I don't feel any anger or confusion about earlier. I just see her, naked in the twilight, her eyes dark and shaded.

"Something's changed," she says. "But you won't believe me."

"Try me."

She looks down at the grass with a hint of a grin, a young woman with a secret hope that she wants to share but doesn't want to curse.

"It's the moon."

"What about it?"

"I can feel it. When I close my eyes. I know where it is. Right now. I know where it is."

"Where is it?"

"Over there," she says, smitten, pointing diagonally down at the grass and presumably through the planet and out the other side.

"How?" I say, looking around at the sky, making sure it's not visible. It isn't.

"There's a shift in pressure, a lack of gravity, in its direction."

"Maybe it's real."

"It is."

"My grandad could tell you if it was going to rain when he woke up. Said he could feel how heavy the clouds were."

"It's sort of like that. I... I don't know if I should say."

"No. Please. I want you to share this stuff with me."

"I can feel a tunnel, like I'm boring towards it, when I meditate. Digging through space."

"A tunnel? To the moon?"

"Yes."

"And what do you think will happen when you get there?"

"I don't know. Maybe I'll hear its voice. Properly. Clearly."

"Like when you were little?"

"Things are beginning to slip through. Little messages."

"Like the meat thing?"

"Instructions. On how to get there."

"I want to help you get there."

"I know you do. Shall we try?"

"Sure."

"Take off your clothes."

I do as she says and sit back down in my boxer shorts. The air is mild against my back, soothing after being under the hot sun all day. Farzaneh reaches over and traces her fingertips down my chest. I interpret this as an act of reparation, a moment of contact in return for pushing my friends away. She is trying to apologise. I'm agitated to hold her, clutch her and pull her towards me but I resist. She looks up at the sky and inhales deeply.

"Close your eyes," she says, closing her own. "Visualise a tiny white light at the bottom of your spine. Let it radiate across your pelvis. Travel down into it."

I focus on her voice, trying to see the white light she's talking about, but all I see is darkness.

"Feel yourself moving towards the light. Let it open up. Let the path get wider and deeper. Move slowly, forwards. Deeper and deeper. Further and further into it."

Her voice fades away. I open my eyes, cheating, a bad meditator, and see that she is fully immersed in her inner world. Sitting around seeing inner light isn't something I'm capable of. It doesn't present itself to me, not after a few drinks and a couple of joints; it would take more than that.

My mind is too restless, too easily bored. I sit in the garden, eyes obediently closed again, seeing nothing. My head lolls down a couple of times, my jaw jarring against my collar bone and waking me. Meditation is tedium. I'm in a stoned blur, the temperature dropping around me, the stinging pink burn on my thighs deepening.

Farzaneh gasps for air.

"What is it?" I ask, roused by the shift in her respiration.

"I was close," she says, her chest rising and falling, her left hand over her heart.

"Close to what?"

"The light. It split into seven white moons. I think it was a sign. Did you see it?"

"No." I say, shaking my head. "Sorry."

Her eyebrows furrow.

"I felt like you were there," she says. "Somewhere. In the space around me."

She seems sincere. Her eyes are fixed on mine. Our collars are squared. She is here, communicating with me, inviting me into her realm of experience. I nod.

"What was it like?" I ask.

"It was beautiful."

SIX

Farzaneh meditates on the lawn while I sit on a garden chair in the shade of the conifers, trying to get ahead on my course's recommended reading. Sunlight splits through the trees, setting my pages ablaze, making the sharp black font of a difficult Gottlob Frege translation dance in front of my eyes. I move my chair deeper into the shade and push on. The book is like *Theaetetus* without the charisma. It tip-toes around the idea of compositionality, pretending that words have the same ends as numbers, as though the full stop at the end of each paragraph is an equals sign and the invisible answer is sitting on the empty part of the line. It feels incomplete somehow, but I can't put my finger on why. Maybe I'm not concentrating, or I'm too keen on Plato. I decide to break off and prepare some food.

"Lunch-time," I whisper, placating Farzaneh's inner search, putting the plates down on a picnic blanket I've laid on the lawn.

Farzaneh squints at the brightness of the yellow-white light on the grass and shuffles over to the edge of the blanket. We silently eat baba ganoush, sliced carrots and Turkish flat bread while the sky clouds over. The garden is shaded and cool by the time we finish so we shift to the front room, me reading on the couch and Farzaneh meditating on the hardwood floor.

We have spent a lot of the summer out in the garden so I'm only just beginning to realise that our flat has no direct light in it. We descend steps, five feet below street level, to get to our front door. The front window has a bush in front of it, rising up above the shoulders of pedestrians. The back garden has tall conifers. There is a subterranean quality to the space. It is dug out, beneath London. Every room is filled with shade and the sense that darkness prevails.

"You can't spend the rest of your life meditating," I say, with a childish pang, jealous of nothing in particular, just unlooked upon, momentarily anxious that Farzaneh doesn't seem to care about anything in the outside world, least of all me.

"I don't intend to," she says, standing up, ruffled by the interruption.

"What do you intend?"

She ignores this, sits on the opposite end of the couch and starts writing in her notebook, angling it away from me on the inside of her hunched-up thigh. I stare at the blank walls of the living room, remembering the times we spent in her bedsit, lazing around in a sexual stupor, skin touching, stoned but excited, talking about life and ideas. It seems like part of a different existence, with a different person. That version of Farzaneh, with her passions and interests, seemed full of a bottomless energy that would have embraced graduation, gone out into the world, searching and exploring for a way she could add to it all; an outsider, but a contributor. She used to accuse me of being too static and become morbid when we weren't finding new things to do. Now she just sits there meditating, absorbing nothing, radiating nothingness.

"I'm so tense," I say. "Why does it feel like this?"

Farzaneh stops writing and whips a morose glance at me, as though my feelings are petty barriers to better uses of time.

"Like what?" she says.

"You don't have to sit with your knee up like that, for a start."

"I'm writing."

"But you don't have to hide it from me."

"Writing is private. It's a private thing."

"It never used to be. We used to write things together. Or we'd both be writing, openly, next to each other. There were no walls between us. The walls had our writing all over them."

"Sometimes writing is about discovery," she says. "You have to know what something is before you can share it."

"I feel so dull, so weak. I don't feel like me at all. I'm becoming obsessed with how you're feeling, what you're thinking."

She sighs, closes her notebook and starts rubbing her temples.

"You said you were going to be okay with this."

"How am I supposed to understand anything though? You're not telling me what anything means. I don't know where I am with you. You meditate all the time, barely speak. I don't know if all this is still to do with the moon or what."

"Let's go out for a walk. There's something I need to find."

"Yes," I say. "I really need to get away from these bare walls."

Farzaneh looks around at the walls as though their bareness hadn't occurred to her.

We walk through London Fields and down Broadway Market. Farzaneh leads, slipping through the crowd, away from me. I am superfluous, unsure where we are heading. I trail her down the canal for half an hour as cyclists pass on the right and struggle to keep up as she strides through the estates. In Tower Hamlets Cemetery her pace finally slows. Nobody has been buried here since the seventies. It's more of a nature reserve than a graveyard; people walking dogs, wandering couples, young men on benches smoking joints or drinking cans of beer. The ambience is in constant flux between being a respite from the urban sprawl and an overgrown, forgotten about place of death.

"I'm going to stop eating some more things," says Farzaneh.

"What kind of things?"

We turn down a path lined with cypress trees and sarcophaguses as the sun breaks through the clouds. There are two crows walking on the ground ahead with white light bouncing off their backs. Farzaneh has the same white light gleaming on the surface of her eyes. There's an impenetrable purity in it, a serene defence.

"That bread we ate today really clouded my mind. From now on, I only want to eat things that are part of the natural cycle. Things that you can eat when you find them."

"I don't know if you're aware but there was an agricultural revolution that interrupted the natural cycle about twelve thousand years ago."

"I'm not talking about farming."

"I don't think anybody has *found* a carrot since the sixteen forties."

"Cynicism doesn't suit you."

"So, don't inspire it."

"It just has to be part of nature. Nothing processed or chemically treated."

"Fine. Organic foods. New menu. Got it."

"Good," she says, resting her hand on my shoulder for a second, relieved now that she has got her dietary changes off her chest. "I'm so glad."

"I wish you'd share more, about what you're thinking, where all this stuff is coming from."

"There's nothing to share. It's nature. Instinct. That's the whole point."

"But you must reflect on it. When you meditate."

"No. That's something else."

We carry on walking. Stone angels stand dismembered and decapitated among hanging willow branches. Cremation stones are left forgotten, piled in corners, overrun with weeds. The ground is uneven and has given way so dramatically in some areas that the tombs have burst open. Some of the plots are lost to wild growth, dilapidated and impenetrable.

"The light here is beautiful," she says, "pouring through the gaps in the trees. Don't you think?"

"Sure."

"Sometimes I think light can undo the distance between the inside and the outside. Its energy connects the mind and the body and the world."

I imagine Farzaneh's mind and body converging with light and space, becoming them, them becoming her, unfathomable electrical bridges colliding and twisting together. Nothing like that happens inside of me.

"I feel like I'm losing you," I say.

"You're not. I'm here. It's just hard. This whole thing, trying to reconnect, when I'm always being pulled back. I'm glad you're here. I am. But you have to try harder to let me go. You promised."

"I know. I'm sorry."

We walk around the perimeter until we get to a bench that has been spray-painted in a rainbow motif. It looks brash, set against the mud and graves and trees; something acidic and urban standing in the old natural order. Farzaneh stops and sits on it. We stare into the blazing greens of the bush across the path. She seems to have no idea that I'm upset and disturbed by her lack of feeling for our relationship. She is thinking of something else.

"Let's go away," she says. "Before your course starts up again."

"I can't afford to go away."

"I'll pay."

"I don't know."

"Please. Let me spend some of my money on something for both of us."

"A holiday would be nice."

"Good," she says, kissing me on the cheek, then pausing and pulling her lips away. "Seven white moons…"

There is a white tombstone in front of us, standing before

the foliage. Separating the ornamental roof-shaped peak from the memorial stone's epitaph is a band of seven white circles.

"The tombstone?"

"You were with me when I found them," she says. "Of course."

"I don't understand."

"This is the place."

She stands up and walks across the path, past the grave, and lifts the arm of a branch, disappearing into the bushes and hanging creepers beneath some ash trees and young sycamores. I stand up and follow her in. The light is dim. The edges of the trees' sunned, drying leaves rustle and hum in the air in all directions. There are a couple of passageways. I follow the one from which I can hear snapping twigs and rattling leaves. Thick thorny weeds and nettles scratch at my jeans and thin branches and creepers break across my forearms and chest. I yank and pull my way into a domed circular clearing, a cave of sorts, a few metres wide and almost tall enough to stand up in. Farzaneh is sitting in the middle of it with her legs crossed.

"This is it," she says, unusually happy. "This is the place the moon told me to find."

"This place?"

"Isn't it perfect?"

"It's the middle of a bush, in a graveyard," I say, brushing a spider's web from my neck. "I feel like I'm covered in insects."

"Don't you see? This is a good thing. It means we're supposed to be together. Somehow, I'm supposed to do this with you."

"Okay," I say. "Do what?"

"Do you mind leaving me?" she asks. "Just for a little while. I need to meditate."

SEVEN

Venice is overcrowded and smells of sewage, but the weather, for September, is bright and warm. The streets are full of happy couples indulging in a romantic narrative that Farzaneh considers idiotic and false. I'm not so sure. If love is a story that people tell themselves to feel better about life, plotting trips to Italy and scripting lines about how lucky they are, then it looks like this particular story is enough to keep most people happy. I'm nostalgic for the first three months of our relationship, when people on the street would have thought we looked like we were in love.

The truth is we've never said it out loud, mostly because Farzaneh hates the idea, and I know that if I say it she will reject it. The idea of her condescension, in that moment, looking down on the meaning and motivation of my declaration, is too much for me to face. It gnaws at me though, needing the confirmation, and for some reason I've pegged this trip as the time. It has to be said in Venice.

Farzaneh looks divine in the simple dresses that she's brought with her but she has been distant since we got off the plane. In the Accademia, she walks from picture to picture announcing the surnames of painters as though the whole premise of visiting a gallery is an inane box-ticking exercise.

"Canaletto… Carpaccio… Bellini…"

In the whole place, she only pauses for Tintoretto's

The Miracle of the Slave. The eponymous slave has been condemned for worshipping St Mark. He is collapsed and foreshortened with his legs broken and eyes gouged out, blind and immobile. St Mark's horizontal body is flying providently down to him from heaven. The proscenium of figures makes the appearance of St Mark seem alive with movement. My eyes keep moving over to a man in red on the right. He is the condemner, the Knight of Provence. His accusatory stance, though prominent, is having no impact on the scene. His outburst is being ignored by everyone, part of their shared inhumanity. Their sole focus is witnessing the slave's decimation, and thereby ignoring the miracle. Just as I'm becoming immersed in what the picture has to say about civilisation, Farzaneh moves on, listing artists as she goes:

"Giorgione... Veronese..."

Art used to be one of Farzaneh's deepest inspirations. Discussing paintings helped her to illuminate the idea that underpinning the physical world there was a realm of meaning and beauty. Now, she's acting as though pictures are just pointless representations.

The same disheartened display occurs the next day at the Guggenheim Collection. Nothing rouses her. I walk beside her hoping that, any second, she'll wake from her dulled perceptions and talk with enthusiasm and excitement, like she did when she spoke about these very pictures, showing prints of them to me in books on her bed. Instead, she shuffles on, taking her register of names:

"Magritte... Pollock... Bacon..."

She pauses at a Rothko, finally seeing something. I'm impressed by the scale of it, and his others. They are experiences in colour; six feet wide and towering ten feet up from the floor. They have no deeper resonance for me but I find them pleasurable, and their scale bold. The painting that has arrested Farzaneh's attention has a black base with three large soft-edged blocks of colour. The lowest block is a deep purple almost invisible in the bordering black, the central, largest block is blood red and the slim upper block is moonlight white. Farzaneh stands in front of it for over ten minutes. I don't rush her. I want her to feel something. I circle the room a couple of times and then stand beside her again.

"I like this one too," I say.

Done with it, she moves on to the next room and starts up again:

"Dali... Ernst..."

The next day, we walk around the city. Her breasts, loose in a thin cotton dress, are catching the eyes of lots of men. Husbands ignore their wives as they stare, friends tap each other's shoulders and point with excitement, lovers allow their eyes to slide away from their beloveds. Walking through the narrow streets, sitting at outdoor tables, standing in queues to get inside old churches, everywhere we go, men are bending their necks with their eyes fixed on her. I'm feeling unusually jealous about the attention she's attracting, probably because we haven't had sex in over a week.

We take a ride in a gondola. It's supposed to be the thing that all the happy couples do, part of the narrative of coming here. We're meant to be holding each other, looking into each other's eyes, either too besotted to notice the world around us or pointing out beautiful things and agreeing about them. Farzaneh leans back, her head turned away from me, looking off towards the crumbling buildings on the other side of the canal. The gondolier looks down at her as much as is politely possible and, when he sees that I've noticed, gives me a happy smile, almost congratulatory, one that says well done for being the man who gets to bed this woman. I try to smile back but find myself staring at him with no humour until he turns away.

At lunch in San Marco's square, Farzaneh has somehow attracted a small group of Venetian boys, about fifteen or sixteen years old They are standing outside the gate to the outdoor tables where we're sitting. The Lothario of the group is waving, trying to get her attention. His friends are smiling, laughing, and talking into each other's ears. When he begins cooing at a volume loud enough to be embarrassing, Farzaneh shoos him away with a tiny gesture of her hand. He obliges her and moves his gang along, whistling and twisting his neck as he goes.

I can't even watch the string quartet under the gazebo without noticing the viola player glancing over. There's a building sensation of pressure in my temples and the sinuses around my eyes. When the waiter comes with our bill and proceeds to look fixedly at her breasts with a grateful smile I stand up, the metal chair scraping on the stone floor, and start to leave.

"Where are you going?" she asks.

"For a walk."

"Where?" she calls.

"Anywhere."

I leave her to deal with the bill and wander around trying to get lost, hoping to lose myself by proxy. In shop window after shop window there are hundreds of decorative Venetian masks. The notion of her dead father taking her into one of these stores, telling her to pick out her favourite, twists and knots my thoughts. Farzaneh's ungraspable centre hides behind all of them. The empty eyes glare out at me.

I walk in one direction, crossing bridges over canals, passing through a Jewish quarter, weaving in and out of alleyways until I end up on the edge of the city, looking out to sea towards an island with a stately wall around it. Sea buses are traveling out to it, and then coming back, and the process of watching them moving along the water calms me. I find a Jewish gondolier down some old steps next to a little bridge. He's wearing a black top hat, black suit and has a large but well-trimmed black beard. He looks like Death's gondolier, all but missing an 'end is nigh' sign. I ask him to take me back to the hotel.

Drifting down backstreet canals, I ask myself how I've got to the point where I'm sitting in a gondola on my own in Venice. Happy couples pass by in their boats, and the smell of their perfumes and aftershaves is stronger than the bittersweet septic tank smell of the sinking city. I reflect on how love seems, above all things, to be about two people choosing to overlook life's usual power negotiations, allowing each other in, being grateful for them, accepting them, and letting the wider world melt away. This is why I'm feeling so alone and bitter, I realise, not because I'm jealous of the men who desire Farzaneh, but because she is in her own world and she won't let me in.

I get back to the hotel around dinner time and sit in the restaurant drinking red wine. Being alone where we're supposed to be together, the stress of the day comes back. The wine helps numb the loneliness but not much else. Up in the hotel room, I lie down and start reading the introduction to David Hume's *An Enquiry Concerning Human Understanding*. The language is engaging and better than the other stuff I've been reading on the concept of knowledge but I'm filtering everything in the book through the idea of Farzaneh and her inner journey. My mind drifts through tangents, misty from the wine, and I find myself staring at blurred pages, stalled in my reading. I put the book down on the bedside table and stare at the wall instead.

She comes back to the room around ten o'clock, goes straight into the bathroom and turns on the shower. I grab my book and pretend to read, too late for her to notice. When she leaves the bathroom in a white towel she doesn't ask any questions or volunteer any information. Instead, she slips on a yellow dress that sets off her tanned summer skin, braless again. Her clean, fresh smell breezes into the bedroom and undoes the faecal smell of the streets that has been creeping in through the open window. I want to be the man sitting across the table from this beautiful woman in the yellow dress, making her smile. I shuffle up on my elbows and straighten my spine, about to apologise for leaving her with the bill at lunchtime.

"I'm going for a walk," she says, purposefully mimicking my earlier statement, leaving the room.

I lie back down, roll over onto my face and wrap a pillow around the back of my head, my love for her writhing around in my skull like an angry snake. Having found somebody who makes my life feel rooted in truth, the weight and conviction of my emotions seem emphatic. I don't know what I'd do if she just became more and more distant until she left me. If this was her walking out the door for good, I feel like reality might leave with her.

It's late when she gets back. She slips into bed and puts a hand on my back. I twist my neck, curious. She doesn't say anything. Her hand falls away. I put my head down and roll onto my back, to give her the option to approach me with her body, but she doesn't. She is involved in her own process of getting to sleep and ends up with her back to me.

In the morning, we have breakfast and then wander over to the Rialto Bridge, looking at the little keepsakes, failing to find anything of interest. Immersed in my isolation, Farzaneh in her own world, we go to the Palazzo Ducale and walk through the Great Hall. I glance at *Il Paradiso*, the world's largest oil painting, as if it's a commonplace thing.

"More Tintoretto," says Farzaneh.

The grand pillars and archways don't ignite our interest either. The only point at which we are even nearly roused is on the Bridge of Sighs where, looking through the holes over the sun speckled canal, we both sigh. We glance at each other, acknowledging the synchronicity, how it mirrors the fabled histories of the sighing prisoners who knew that they were never going to see daylight again after crossing the bridge, but our expressions remain flat and untouched.

The next day, walking through an old church, I try to start hushed conversations but nothing gets off the ground. We take a boat trip that goes all the way along the Grand Canal. Somehow, rather than talking to each other, we end up talking to a waiter who works on the boat. He paints a grim picture:

"Venice is sinking, yes, but it is already gone."

"How so?" I ask him.

"You see this cruise ship? Over here. Forty thousand people. Population of Venice, fifty thousand. Four times less than when I was born. There is no space for our way of life now."

"Because of the tourists?"

He nods.

"Every year two thousand Venetians leave, and every year two hundred thousand more tourists arrive. In twenty years, nothing. Like Pompeii. Poof."

"The same thing is happening in London, in a different way. The other side of the stick."

"The stick?"

"Money. Pushing people away."

"Yes," he says, looking over at the cruise ship. "These people have too much."

The boat ends up by a park where we have an hour before we have to get back onboard. Even in her withdrawn state, Farzaneh's walk has a natural flow, a desirability. The curve of her spine has an animalistic dynamism, revealing the unlikely balance of the bipedal form. I momentarily feel that, by touching her, I will make contact with a world that has abandoned me, provoke its beauty and its consciousness, and so I put my hand on her waist and try to kiss her neck. She tilts her head away and shifts her hips, breaking away from me. I have no idea what I'm supposed to be doing or thinking. We still haven't had sex since we got here and my secret hope, that we would declare our love, seems like the furthest thing from her mind.

"What's going on?" I ask.

"What? Nothing."

"Why did you bring me here? What was the point?"

"To show you Venice."

"This holiday has got nothing to do with me. You've made that clear enough. So, tell me, why are we here?"

She spins away from me, about to deny me an explanation, but then slowly turns back.

"I wanted to retrace my steps, get closer to that time. I've even been dressing like I used to dress, when I was little. I'm sorry. But I really did want to do it with you."

"But you've practically ignored me."

"It's hard to focus. The streets are so busy. The memories are all blurred."

"You've made me feel so alone."

Admitting this out loud brings sadness welling up to my eyes. Farzaneh's eyebrows knit together. I can see her sympathy, deep in the tunnels of her eyes, trying to come forward and help me, but the distance is too far. She's hoping that this sorry moment, showing me a hint of empathy, will be enough. And it is. I feel so starved of her that the notion that she's even aware of my suffering is enough. I relax my face and turn the corner of my lips, showing her that I am retreating from my emotional needs. Farzaneh sighs and shifts her weight from one foot to the other.

"There's something else. I think it's affecting us too."

"What?"

"I've been afraid to tell you."

"What is it?"

"I've been stalling, because I know it isn't fair."

"Please, just tell me."

My thoughts shift uncontrollably between two points: she's going to tell me she loves me or she's going to tell me it's over. Why is it possible that it could be either?

"I need to stop having sex," she says.

"Sex?"

"Yes."

"Sex? But why?"

"At first, I thought it might help, because you can really connect with yourself if you do it right, but I've come to realise that it's a false promise, a temporary glance. It only ever leads back to the beginning."

"The beginning of what?"

"The journey."

"So, what comes next?"

"I keep searching, keep going, until I figure this thing out."

"But you want to stay together?"

"Yes. If you want to."

"We don't have to have sex," I say. "I don't care about that. Not in the short term."

"No," she agrees. "We can't."

On our last day, Farzaneh leads us north through a couple of courtyards with small Catholic churches and on into ever narrowing streets. The local shops and cafés are out of business and the windows are shuttered with scrappy black graffiti sprawled across them. The plaster is falling off the walls regularly enough for broken pieces to line the edges of the streets and alleys. The bricks of some of the walls are fully exposed with only scraps of plaster left clinging on. We pass the secluded entrance to a glass workshop, a supplier to the tourist shops closer to town, the smell of burnt sand wafting out. We end up on the edge of the island, surrounded by flower shops, right by where the sea buses leave for that odd-looking island with the ornate wall around it. Farzaneh buys us tickets and raises her eyebrows. There is a little bit of light in her eyes for the first time all week.

The boat is unmoored and the engine growls beneath us. The disturbed sea releases a salty, mossy scent. We find seats near the front where we can see ahead.

"My dad brought me here," she says, nodding toward the island. "It's quiet. Calmer. I don't know why I didn't think of it before."

"What is it?"

"The Isola di San Michele. The Island of the Dead. It's a cemetery. Dad said that the church was, arguably, the first church of the Renaissance."

"It's a strange-looking place."

"Stravinsky is buried here, if I remember correctly, and Ezra Pound."

"Wasn't he a fascist?"

"He was a lot of things."

I nod and look ahead. This is her last stab at reconnecting with her childhood, finding that strange territory of mind she had in the months after her mother died. The boat passes along a path of miniature unlit street lights strapped to trios of logs which rise a couple of feet out of the blue-green water. I watch the island wall begin to swell and broaden as the boat approaches. Giant cypress trees pop up above the top of it.

The boat pulls up near the white marble façade of the San Michele church which overlooks the lagoon. Three old women and a solemn, well-dressed family get off with us, carrying bunches of chrysanthemums. Farzaneh walks through the gate, away from the newer administrative buildings and over towards the church. All the graves have photos of the deceased on the tombstones. It gives the cemetery an extra dimension, the loss of all those Venetian faces.

Farzaneh stops by the old locked up church. After Venice's Gothic architecture and beautiful piazzas, it doesn't look like anything special and we're not standing in the best place to view it but I sense that she has a memory associated with the spot. Her face has simmered away into expressionless remembrance.

"Mortality will outlive immortality," she says to herself, most likely quoting her father.

I reach out and rest my hand on her shoulder. Her whole body becomes rigid. Without a word, she slips from beneath my hand and wanders off through the graves. I wait for a moment, trying to decipher something, anything, from the tone of what she said but just find myself staring at the church. I can see St Michael, the holder of the scales, carved into a marble arch, waiting for Judgement Day.

When I look back, Farzaneh is further away than I imagined. I set out after her, through the graves, but can't seem to catch up. I feel like I'm walking faster but I can't be because she is getting even further ahead. Wincing through the crystal haze of the sunny day, my eyes beginning to water, she looks as though I've dreamt her up. Light spills through her dress, one hand flapped out, fingertips gliding softly over the top of gravestones, the other gently swinging her bag, just a girl. I rub the moisture from my eyes and, as I do, she disappears.

I walk towards where I thought she was but I lose sense of the place. The rows of graves look too uniform, but at the same time none of the lines are straight. Blink or glance away and you don't know where you are. I look back and head away from the church, systematically edging towards a triangulated point where I think she might be, checking down each curved corridor of headstones as I go. When I get to where I think she disappeared there's nothing. She's nowhere.

Then, I notice a tombstone with an almost identical design to the one in Tower Hamlets, crafted over a hundred years ago. This one is brand new, gleaming and white, but with the same seven circles separating the triangular roof from the main rectangular stone. It's five graves across and one row down. As I approach, I see a pile of mud by it. On the near side of the pile there's a hole, six feet deep. I stand over the edge and look down. Farzaneh is lying on her back at the bottom, naked, wearing her white Venetian mask with purple feathers extruding from the edges.

"Farzaneh?" I ask, whispering for some reason.

Looking down into the shadows at the white mask and her naked body, a sorry lust flows through me and I remember that we've agreed to stop having sex. I look around the island, all the way to the shining walls. There is an old widow kneeling by a tombstone about a hundred metres away but no one else in sight.

"Farzaneh?"

"Come down," she says, words slipping out from behind the mask's still lips. "I can really feel it down here."

I scan the surrounding area again and hesitantly lower myself down into the hole. Farzaneh sits up and crosses her legs. I sit down facing her at the opposite end of the grave. The pressure in the air is heavier. A couple of hundred metres to the side and we would be in the sea. It smells dusty and infertile, slightly salty. My head feels like it's submerged in weightless water. The air tastes dry and shadowy.

"Are you going to keep that on?" I ask, referring to the mask.

"Yes."

"What are we doing down here?"

"Didn't you see the gravestone?"

"The circles?"

"Moons."

"I think it's just a common motif."

"There's no harm in a little superstition. It's where the deepest voices hide. Meditate with me."

"I'll try."

I close my eyes and see the black eyes of the mask dancing around a sunspot in my mind. I don't know how I got it into my head that this was going to be the holiday where we declared our love for each other. I have to accept that to be with Farzaneh is also to accept that love, as I know it, isn't part of her perceived experience. That is not to say that she is missing an essential part of her being, or that she is broken in some way. In Farzaneh's world, grief has revealed depths of feeling and experience that I can't imagine. If anything, her perspective should have the power to subvert my own idea of love, open me to the complexities of the emotions and how they make us reinterpret reality, maybe even admit that the love that I desire might reflect a missing part in me, or that I am too eager to play a role that society has told me is inevitable.

I chase the eyes of the mask deeper into myself, trying to find a declaration that matches who we are more precisely. Not love, something else. I sense that there is something meaningful that we share, a truth as powerful as love, but I lack the vision to illuminate it. I only find empty reflection, the eyes of the mask dispersed into darkness. Dead bodies linger in the walls around me, perhaps only inches away through the soil. Their truths forgotten. Their hopes lost.

PART THREE

ONE

We are in Shoreditch for a Poetry Slam at a place called the Neon Sympathy near Hoxton Square. They sell craft ales, cocktails and gourmet bar snacks and have an abundance of sharp-dressed, well-trained staff. It's a money-minded place where the management expects its nervous but cool events team to fill the three-hundred-capacity venue every night. Their monthly 'Poetry Slam' is trying to capitalise on the mass-market appeal of the recent spate of spoken word poetry from South London that mixes the confessional style with hip-hop's focus on self-knowledge and protest. They have put boards covered in graffiti on the stage and lit it like a New York comedy club. Farzaneh is drinking a glass of tap water with a scowl on her face, impatiently waiting for the event to start. I'm holding an Old Fashioned that was so expensive I hardly dare sip it.

In her introduction, the young woman who has taken to the stage is repeatedly and stutteringly apologetic about her existence so the two hundred people who have paid eight pounds to get in are happy to ignore her and keep drinking and chatting. Seemingly, for most of them, the venue is just a bar near work with a cheap enough door price. At most, they want to tell their friends and colleagues they went to *see* poetry last night. Omitting the listening part.

Farzaneh hustles forward and sits at a small round table closer to the stage so that she can hear the poet. I follow and sit down with her. A handful of others move towards the tables too. With a group of around twenty people showing a vested interest, the poet takes a worried glance at the crowd and decides to begin. Her nervousness grows into a weak, frenetic passion as she reads her work and this puts the people paying attention at ease. At least we can hear her over the crowd. Her jittering intensity even quietens a few people behind us but the overall ambience is still burlesque with post-work banter and chatter.

Her poems are abstract musings on identity politics and LGBT life in London. They aspire to being slammed but are in danger of being wet and confessional. She is a woe-is-me outsider. Suburban angst keeps creeping through, and a sense of victimhood. "This may be my most lesbian poem," she says, to a few polite laughs, before reading her final piece. She paints a picture in which her clitoris is a buoy on an ocean of experiences, coming into contact with various kinds of weather, creatures and vessels. The image system is solid and well crafted. Her message is one of cowardly solitude and an inability to submerge into a more profound and dangerous experience. We clap for what is her best and most honest work as she leaves the stage.

Next up the steps is an obese American man, escaped from the rust belt, now painting his fingernails different colours, wearing bright paisley scarves, and eating cheeseburgers in London. His work is about the backward ways of America's Jesus-loving, gun toting hate-criminals and how you can never leave the town where you grew up. He is hungry for every single ear and, knowing how to oscillate his voice to break people's inattention, soon has two-thirds of the crowd listening to his surreal re-imaginings of violence, rape and murder in the Midwest.

He chats between poems with the knowing air of a stand-up comedian. A confused amusement flows around the crowd.

They are pleased and repelled by him in equal measure. They want to believe his stories but they don't. They want to be liberal enough to accept his difference but they aren't. He has a bold and brazen ego that they were eager to listen to for a few minutes but now they're desperate to get away from him for the rest of time. Still, they listen because his strange peacock clothing and his shrill voice conjure the exotic, instilling superstitious fears, a sense that if they talk over him he will throw his voice in their direction and it will rip them in two for everyone to see.

He talks about the inspiration for his final poem for five minutes before reading it. Farzaneh is up next, shuffling a small pile of A4 paper, ordering and reordering. Her hands and wrists move sharply. I place my hand on her thigh but she doesn't seem to notice its physical weight or the support its presence implies.

"You're going to be great," I whisper, leaning over.

She looks at me with disdain.

"I don't care about being great."

"Okay, you're going to be whatever you want to be."

"Could you take your hand off me, please?"

"Sorry."

"It's fine."

"Thank you for doing this. I think it's important to put yourself out there. You've been so boxed in."

"I don't understand what you think reading poems in public is going to do for me."

"Isn't this why people write poetry, to share it?"

"It's not why I write it."

"So, why do you spend so many hours editing it?"

"Because I want to like what I've done. I don't pretend to myself that I'm any good."

"We can go if you like? There's still time."

"No. I owe you this."

"You don't owe me anything."

"I do. We both know I do."

The American guy's voice screeches and shakes as he approaches his final lines. I can barely hear the words. Lots of anger dressed up as wit, vanity dressed up as empathy, talent dressed up as genius. The crowd applauds. He basks in it, decidedly not leaving the stage, raising his hand to salute and prolong the validation, fanning his wet face with the papers his poems are printed on.

A young bearded man in black is beckoning towards Farzaneh from the side of the stage, trying to catch her eye and get her moving to try to keep the goodwill of the crowd alive. Farzaneh is ignoring him, looking blankly ahead, her poems curled up in her hands. She leans her head back on her neck, takes a deep breath and then stands and walks over.

I reach out after her as though there was some vital moment of intimacy that I was denied and then pull my hand back. Farzaneh doesn't acknowledge the American poet as they pass at the foot of the stage and her lack of adulation has an immediate darkening effect, pulling him from the pride-swollen centre-of-the-stage universe back down to the invisible anonymity of the city.

Farzaneh stands at the microphone, dispassionate, a white spotlight on her. The light catches her cheekbones in a way that makes me realise that she has lost a lot of weight. She has an artistic boniness. She looks like somebody who neglects the body but feeds the mind. There is blackness in her eyes, a deathly power given to her by the separation of crowd and stage. She doesn't introduce herself or try to catch anybody's eye, she just steps towards the microphone and begins.

"Passion

Passion is the pursuit of the lonely
Desperate bodies chasing sensations
Chemical chains in the just-here world
Petty drama of catalyst and reaction"

This short, glum poem, purposeful in its affront against normal people's feelings, loses over half of the audience. Their own unedited thoughts are suddenly more interesting to them than Farzaneh's considered stanza. The crowd noise doubles and then doubles again in seconds. Farzaneh shows no emotion, just a dead-eyed gaze into the space above them. She begins to read her next poem.

"To the Moon and Back

We grew up in an age
Where fathers told their daughters
They loved them
To the moon and back
Teaching them
That love is a lot of distance
To conceive of it
You must think remote from yourself
About how far you are willing to go

Imagine
Flying
Two hundred and thirty-nine thousand miles
And two hundred and thirty-nine thousand miles back
To show a child
Who conceives only time
That a journey into absence
Is the extent of your love"

I'm moved by this one, and indignant at the crowd's blasé attitude towards her. Farzaneh's poetry has an intensity that they're ignoring. I wonder if it's more powerful to me, knowing that her father is dead. People are looking at their phones, standing with their backs to her, laughing. She carries on.

"New Moon

In your first phase
Again
Your elliptical longitude
The same as the sun's
You are invisible
In silhouette
Bathing
In earthshine
Twelve hours later
Than last time
When you were three hours earlier
Than the time before that
Nobody
Can quite map
Exactly when you'll disappear
An eccentric orbit
They call it
Nanoseconds of loss
Hours of negation
Outside the metre
Of mathematics
People think
You are trapped
Enslaved
In our service
But I know
You are flying
You are free"

I produce a single clap then remember that nobody has been applauding between poems. I'm not sure how many she intended to read but she brought around ten with her. I'm probably biased but her language seems cohesive, and her meanings are the right amount clear and the right amount opaque. She is giving me hope that there's something in the world for her, something for her to aspire to. Reading seems to be having the opposite effect on Farzaneh but she flips the page regardless. She seems to flick her eyes towards me for a second, take an extra beat. My focus sharpens. She begins to read.

"The Distances Involved

My mother's heart ran away. Volume too loud. Colours too bright. Everybody getting at her. Secret conspiracies, closer and closer, pecking at her brain. Everything too near. Too pestering. Too frantically local. In the end, she tried to throw herself out of a window. It wasn't as close as it seemed. That glass. She failed. Managed to land in an institution. Sat silent and mortified in bed. Ashamed of her shortcomings. Gone. Nothing could bring her back. No number of husband's tears. No confused daughter. Not even a building with pre-cut food. In the toilet, where the walls were near, she stuffed tissues down her throat until her face turned blue.

My father's heart was always trying to get closer. To his grief. To love. To me. Everywhere there were connections. Opportunities to bond. Even in cancer, his furthering mind reached out. Making sure everything remained near. 'Far,' he would say, urgently, eyes wide but blind, like a visionary seeing a prophetic future in a film. 'Far.' Hand out. Reaching for me. My arm. My shoulder. Once my breast. Hadn't called me 'Far' much before. Could have been saving time. To get nearer. Quicker. But the word looked to report his journey. Explained the distances involved. Said, sorry, poor daughter. It's impossible to stay. The path back becomes longer. Death is a kind of displacement."

173

My eyes are welling and my throat feels like it's closing, so tight I can barely breathe. This is the first time I have heard any intimate details about her parents' deaths. I'm desperate to hold her. Comfort her. Was this the only way she could tell me? Did she even think about the fact that she hadn't told me? As the full gravity of her grief is beginning to dawn on me, and I struggle to keep my sorrow in, Farzaneh looks around at the noisy crowd. This, seemingly, is exactly how important she imagined her poetry would be to people. Even at her most confessional, aligned with the version of poetry that this format most demands and rewards, the crowd remains distracted and self-regarding. I can see in her eyes that she feels that they have rejected the very concept of emotion, and the chance to connect. They are a red-cheeked, shiny-skinned ugly mass of animal flesh. Farzaneh grabs the microphone with a violent motion, screwing up her poems in her fist. She bends her spine, lowers her eyes onto the crowd and yells:

"I am the moon's favourite one! I am the moon's favourite one! I am the moon's favourite one!"

Unlike her poems, this outburst wins her the attention of the entire room. Everybody looks at her, a little put out by the interruption, wondering if the noise is going to go on for long, but she has already stopped. Slightly baffled, almost with a shrug, the crowd claps for a few seconds and then goes back to talking. Wild-eyed, Farzaneh stomps offstage and strides towards the exit. I get up and follow her out onto the street.

"I'm sorry," she says, agitated, her wrist shaking up by her face, her hand struggling to express her feeling. "I just can't do it. I can't be what you want me to be."

She can't stand still. She is stepping back and forth, twisting side to side. I take her by the shoulders.

"You can. You are."

"I hate poetry."

"It's the crowd, not the poetry."

She turns her shoulders out from my hands.

"It isn't the crowd. It's words. They don't change anything."

"Remember when you told me that all your best friends were dead poets? And I said the same thing about philosophers."

"It's not enough. I don't belong here. None of this is for me."

"You're just going through a rough patch."

"Everything that should be meaningful is meaningless to me."

"Not everything…"

She looks at me with the creak of an apology slipping through.

"I'm sick of disappointing you."

"You're not," I say. "You couldn't."

"I can't do it anymore. I just have to go all in."

"You're talking about the moon."

"Yes."

"Come on," I say, putting my hand on her upper arm. "You struggle but you do feel things, underneath it all. You need to see beyond this moon thing once in a while."

"No," she says, brushing my hand off. "I need you to stop touching me."

"What?"

"I'm serious. I need to stop feeling you on my skin."

"I think that might be the worst thing you've ever said to me."

"I don't want things to touch me anymore. Not for a while."

I look around. The post-work drinkers are in their wobbling, leering stride, screeching and laughing, eating, drinking and smoking on the street. Cars, buses, motorbikes and cyclists are fighting for space and motion on the roads. Headlights and brake lights and shop signs blaze in the darkness. Farzaneh, standing before this typically busy London scene, is my point of focus, my stability in the chaos.

"If that's what you need," I say, "I'll stop touching you."

She looks up to the sky, exasperated with my patience, then squats down low and puts her hands on her head. Her pelvis starts writhing and swinging while she moves her fingertips around on her scalp. Her motions coil and intensify until her legs and spine spring up straight and she screams, screeching, high and loud, a piercing plea for annihilation up into the night sky.

The remnants of the white noise from the venue's speakers and her high-end shriek tear open an empty space in the centre of my ear drums and a massive living blackness opens in my mind, a momentary infinity, a deeper consciousness, the source of something in Farzaneh transferred into a hidden primacy in me. The pores and hairs on my spine rise up. The back of my neck is covered with fizzing activity. Then her scream ends and the black energy fades and turns to nothing.

I'm left looking at her, limp and full of her anguish. The nearby drunks have stopped to stare at her. I have never seen somebody look more separate from the rest of the world, and never felt somebody else's solitude more deeply in myself. I struggle to resist embracing her. Her lonely universe is in me and now, more than ever before, I have a lingering belief that Farzaneh isn't indulging herself in a neurosis. She is and needs to be in contact with a portion of existence that I don't understand.

TWO

The people on my course are becoming more friendly and familiar. Their tight, nipped faces are unfurling and I'm perceiving, in their newfound receptivity, a sorry sense of loss for all the connections that we didn't share. I imagine it reflects their fear of the wider world, the notion that their freedom to learn and ruminate on their identities is coming to an end. Within months they will have to make definitive choices based on self-sufficiency and survival. They are exposed, before the city, sky-high walls speeding towards them, and they are seeking each other, finally reaching out, hoping to come together in a final flurry of youth and activity.

I'm scared of graduating too but it isn't making me friendlier. It's making me more critical of my weak-hearted course mates who could have reached out to me two years ago when I was trying to make eye-contact, struggling to start conversations about books and essays in corridors, watching them walk away without my contact details. I hung out with a few of the less guarded of them and I've been rewarding these particular people by accepting their invitations: Turkish tea and baklava with a view to discussing ancient Mediterranean cultures, smoking flavoured tobacco through hookahs while deconstructing the *Tibetan Book of the Dead*, taking a tour of historical points of interest relating to the punk movement while discussing the history of nihilism and anarchy in London. All this time, if I'd only known, I should have been approaching third-year students to find the experiences I wanted.

The library is cold and the three guys I came with who are also writing their dissertations on Sartre have dropped the concept of bad faith for a computer game called *The Last Man*, one of them insisting that it's based on Mary Shelley's post-apocalyptic plague novel of the same name. I give up on a dense page of *Being and Nothingness* that I've been reading and re-reading for the past half hour. Does existence precede essence? The more I ask myself this question the less I know what it means. Philosophy is beginning to seem like an indulgence, a way of using lots of time and effort to express something that everybody else can say in a few words. Just as I'm closing in on the idea of Existentialism, about to write tens of thousands of words about it, I'm thinking more about the fact that each branch of philosophy is just an authorial meta-fiction. All the books and theories I've read are just stories without narratives, worlds without locations, characters without actions. The idea of putting the next three or four months of my life into writing an essay that explains just one of them seems pointless, part of an analytical tradition that obscures reality. Being able to understand a stream of logic isn't going to be relevant when the money from my final loan cheque runs out.

I shove my books in my bag and message Jake. He reluctantly agrees to brave the snow and meet up for a coffee. It's the first time snow has stuck to the ground in London since I've been here. On the streets, most of it is being trodden and driven into oblivion as soon as it lands but it's covering the rooftops and trees, and sticking in the parks. We meet at the café by the lake in Victoria Park. The water has frozen over. I've forgotten to wear a hat and my head is aching from the ears in. Jake is holding two take-out coffees with his shoulders hunched and his nose hovering over one of the cups. He holds one out for me as I approach. I take it and nod my thanks.

"Why the hell are we outside?" he asks.

"To get away from our dissertations."

"We could do that inside."

"Look at it though."

He looks through the falling snow, out across the frozen lake, over at a cluster of parents who have brought their toddlers and small children out, past them to a group of teenage truants squealing and laughing as they throw snowballs at each other. The grass is white, the bare trees' branches are steeped in white, the boundary gate is ridged with white, the roofs of the houses beyond are white, the sky above them is white.

"It's too white," he says, reaching into his pocket for his sunglasses and putting them on. "Don't suppose you've brought a spliff?"

"I thought downers were for downers?"

"They are."

"I didn't."

"Damn it."

"Let's keep moving."

We walk along the path. The day's snow has mostly covered the morning school children and worker's footsteps. It crunches and breaks underfoot, not yet icy or slippery. There are pristine portions of grass where no feet or dogs have wandered.

"How are things? It's been ages."

"Terrible," he says. "Miserable."

I smile.

"Why? What's going on?"

"To be honest, I think the drugs are making me depressed. Or maybe I've got seasonal affective disorder or something. I feel like shit, all the time. I've been having these insane moments, pranging out in bed, completely losing my grip, falling into this creepy vortex It's kind of fucked."

"Take a break. Sounds like you've been partying too hard."

"I can't. Yola. She's a machine. She just wants to get on it all the time."

"It doesn't mean you have to."

"It does. I don't know why but it does. When I'm with her, I want whatever she wants."

"It must be what you want too, on some level."

"Did I tell you she quit her course?"

"The occupational therapy? No."

"Hated her placements. Said the whole thing made her too sad, society was too sick. Helping people was only going to delay the *new world*. We're living in this filthy warehouse with a bunch of delusional hipster-hippies. They all hate me because I want to make money. One guy thinks I'm a spy."

"I can't believe she quit her course so close to the end. That's a lot of debt to come out with nothing."

"These wreck-heads in the warehouse, all they believe in is raving and the end of capitalism. They don't want to do anything with their lives. They're all lazy. Yola makes things happen. She's a doer. But it's just parties. Party after party."

"Maybe she'd think about making other things happen if you told her how you feel."

"But these losers she wants to spend all her time with... I don't want her to make things happen for them. I don't want their world to happen."

"Maybe she just wants to escape for a little while. Doesn't feel ready for the real world quite yet. She can always finish her degree later."

"They're all scared. They want their safe little utopia, with no responsibilities, an out-of-your-mind experience, where nobody has to grow up, and everything feels good, until the next day, and the five days after that, when they all feel grim and destroyed and sit around smoking rollies, staring at walls. Sorry. I'm ranting."

"It's fine. I like your rants."

"I realise that I'm basically expressing exactly what Farzaneh said last summer."

"Not far off."

"I thought she was being a dick. Because I could see that

she was pulling us apart. You and me. She didn't want other people around. But some of what she was saying was more insightful than I gave her credit for."

"Do you know what it sounds like to me?"

"What?"

"Transference."

"Transference of what?"

"You're blaming these warehouse guys instead of Yola, so you don't have to be angry with her, because you're afraid of the confrontation. And that's really unlike you."

"It's different with her. I can't explain it."

"Maybe you think it might be over? But you don't want to face it."

"I could never leave her. The lifestyle can't be for ever. I know that. But I know I can't live without her."

"You're stuck with the idiots then."

"What about you and Farzaneh? Still together?"

"Whatever together means."

"Oh? I heard she'd gone."

"Gone? Gone where?"

"I don't know. Someone said she'd gone."

"She's not gone. She's with me. She's at home."

"Why so touchy?"

"Things aren't easy."

"Were they ever?"

"At the start," I say, catching his eye. "We haven't had sex in months."

"Yola's worn mine down to a nub."

"You always had a way with words."

"I can barely keep up."

"Farzaneh won't even let me touch her."

"It's probably just a dry spell."

"It's more than that. But it's hard to explain."

"You want to get into it?"

"No. It's fine. I'm bored of thinking about it. Where's this warehouse you're in? I thought all those sorts of places had been renovated by now."

"There are still a few about, here and there. A bit further out than anyone with a job in the city would like. And they're hard to get into, but there's been an exodus to Berlin. People escaping the rent. An offer popped up."

"Why not just get a little flat and go to somebody else's warehouse at the weekend?"

"She wants to feel part of something."

"But what if she isn't?"

"Maybe she's right though. Not for me. I'll be able to make money. But for those guys, I don't know… Say you're working in a coffee shop earning twenty thousand a year, when it costs four hundred thousand for a tiny one-bedroom flat five miles from the centre. If you can afford to spend half your wage on your mortgage, that's forty years, without interest, and that's presuming you have the ten per cent deposit to get your foot on the ladder. But, if you don't, how much do you think you can save a month, spending fifty percent of your wage on rent, minus food and bills and travel? One hundred? Two hundred quid? Let's say one fifty. How long before you've got your forty-k deposit? About twenty years? That's sixty years of work for a one-bedroom flat, retiring in your eighties, with all the interest left to pay. I mean, in this scenario, you can't have a family, or buy a car, or go on holiday. To buy an actual house, with bedrooms for children, you have to be a millionaire. From their position, it's unfathomable. Wouldn't you rather just fuck it off and pretend that dancing might save the world?"

"Please. You're depressing me now. Besides, there's nothing wrong with renting. Who cares if a bunch of bastards own all the houses? Let them waste their lives thinking about which Audi to buy."

"But property is theft, man," he says, in a bad hippy parody. "We have to lynch the landlords."

"You need to get out of that warehouse."

We sip our coffees and cross the road that splits the park, walking into the northern half.

"This side of the park is always bigger than I remember."

"It's a serious bit of land. Almost surprising the council haven't sold it off."

"They rent most of it out for festivals during the summer though. It stops being public land at that point. So, they're on the way."

"True. People want their overpriced festivals though."

"Also true."

We crunch through the snow, our coffee cups empty.

"What's going on with Farzaneh then? She still seeking her *deeper truth*? Yola didn't shut up about that for weeks by the way."

"All she does is meditate. For months now. And she's refusing to eat so much stuff."

"You would not believe some of the dietary requirements in the warehouse."

"But I love her. You know? I'd do anything— What's that?"

I point over towards a bush across some pristine snow. There's a clump of black ice with a pale blue football scarf trailing out. I start walking towards it. Jake follows.

"Maybe the park rangers pulled down a snowman."

"Why would they do that?"

"Who knows why park rangers do the things they do?"

"I imagine they're all in a little hut somewhere, drinking tea, waiting it out."

"Zero-hour summer contracts, more like."

At the bush, I squat down. The scarf is a Manchester City football scarf; Jake's team, if he still considers them that. I haven't seen him in his football shirt since he met Yola. I follow the line of the scarf into the undergrowth where a pallid, bearded face lies open-mouthed and open-eyed.

"It's a dead guy."

"Shut up," laughs Jake, bending down. "It's not a dead guy... Oh shit. Give him a nudge."

"He's frozen solid. I'm not touching a dead body."

"Move over."

Jake edges in for a closer look.

"Well?"

"Looks like he's only in his thirties."

"Dead?"

"Definitely dead."

I call the emergency services. My hand begins to freeze as the operator tries to find out where we are in the park in relation to a road map and I, not knowing the road names, try to explain our position in terms of what we're near to in the park. In the end, she asks permission to track my location. I say yes and technology takes over. After forty seconds of silence, she says the police and an ambulance are on their way. Jake is still bending over, looking at the dead guy's face when I hang up.

"He doesn't look homeless," he says. "Maybe he was drunk, on his way home."

"Maybe he joined a party collective before he graduated."

"Come on. That's not funny."

"What? It's probably drugs. Right?"

I bend down beside Jake and look at the dead man's face.

"Probably," he says.

"Still human though."

"Yeah."

My right hand, in my pocket, still has the frozen pain of the phone call in it. My nose is numb and my ears ache. I try to imagine the all-over coldness that the dead man must have felt. The pain in my hand and ears, everywhere. Piercing in, tighter and tighter, until his entire body was one giant pin prick, a black point of pressure in a universe of cold. His blood turning to an icy slush. His heart growing slower with every chilly pump.

"Do you think there's anything more?" I ask. "Or do you think you just die under a bush and that's that?"

Jake puts his hands on his knees and stands up. He is disturbed but tries for levity.

"I've had some pretty convincing out-of-body experiences in the last year or two but he's just so dead, isn't he? Dead is dead."

"It feels like a bad omen, finding a dead guy. Don't you think?"

"No. It feels like finding a dead guy. Did they say how long?"

"They're here already, look."

A policewoman and a policeman walk up from the park gates towards us. We tell them what little we know. A couple of medics arrive soon after. A dog walker comes over. Then another. The police look for foul play and clues before deciding to go ahead and pull him out. We watch them break chunks of ice and snow away and then pull the body out from under the bush. We listen to them reporting the event on their radios. Nobody is moved by his death. The city claims people every day. Our feet are getting cold. We move on.

THREE

The restaurant has been quiet all night. Its low-volume classical music, faux-coliseum pillars and plastic creepers are losing sway with the increasingly niche tastes of the local restaurant goers. Less than five minutes' walk away, there are two new pizzerias serving sourdough pizzas with obscure neo-culinary toppings. Their décor is minimal/rustic, their playlists are eclectic and, even though their pizza sauce is bland and their alcohol is aggressively marked up, they are both always brimming with people. We haven't had to open the door to the downstairs tables for over two months.

Tonight is my last shift. I've been working here on and off for two years. Nino, the manager, has his thick hairy arm around my shoulders. He is tactile and emotional, brought up in a family where the men hold each other's hands and face each other while they talk. The restaurant is a family business and the students he takes on as waiters become an extension of that family in his eyes. He has given me a glass of red wine and has been topping it up all night. My leaving has triggered a worried, paternal streak in him.

"You should stay," he says. "Until you find your feet."

Nino's stomach is bulbous. I've rarely been this close to him so my eyes are fixated on it.

"I need time to figure things out."

"There is no time. You need money, no?"

"Did you ever notice that everyone in the restaurant who can live off their wages also lives upstairs with you?"

"Not enough. I know. And yet you look around, you see the nice cars and the delivery trucks. Money everywhere."

"I wouldn't have survived without this place. I'm going to miss it."

He squeezes my shoulder and pivots us round towards a small table by the window, facing two of the six customers in the restaurant.

"Look at this couple over here. Every week they come. Do you think they are in love?"

"I don't know."

"Look at them. This is my lesson to you."

"They seem fine."

"Yes. Fine. We have our ups. We have our downs. But these are lonely people. Not in love."

"Maybe they're just dull. Well-suited dull people."

"There is no dull in love. Love turns you into family. Always caring. Caring is anger and sadness too. Never dull. You understand?"

"Sure."

"Your lady?"

"She's not dull."

"She makes you feel something?"

"Yes."

"Every day?"

"Yes."

"And you make her feel something?"

"I think so. It's harder for some people."

"People are the same. If it's right, they care."

"Not always," I say. "People have things they're going through. It's not always possible to care."

He thinks about this, looking up, as though his mind is chewing on the statement to find out its flavour, then he nods, double taps my shoulder and squeezes me to him.

"A thoughtful boy. Graceful too. You make a good waiter. You should stay. Just a month. Maybe two."

There are three heavy thuds on the restaurant window. Farzaneh is standing on the other side of the glass, her eyes wide with excitement. She bangs on the glass again.

"Sorry, Nino. Let me just see what she wants."

"You're leaving?"

"One minute."

As I walk out onto the street, Farzaneh turns and strides away. I rush after her.

"Far? What is it? What's happening?"

She stops and faces me, holding out her hands. I look down. She's cupping a spherical white stone the size of a paperweight. It is dull, like unpolished marble, with light grey patches; unmistakably moonlike, confusingly moonlike. Her expression is buoyant and eager but silent, exclaiming that this object surely speaks for itself. I find myself in a fleeting reminiscence, not about the good times but the tough times, when Farzaneh allowed her feelings to form walls between us, and the emotional separation filled me with anxiety and despair, until a crack appeared and her feelings started trickling through, and then she would suddenly break down and her truth would come gushing out. We could reconnect from there. Hold each other. Make love. Struggle on. But here, now, holding out this moonstone, I have no idea what kind of truth she is offering me. There's no emotional wall. We're in completely different worlds.

"What is it?" I ask, determined not to mention the stone's moonlike qualities.

"It came from the moon," she says.

"What do you mean it came from the moon?"

She sets off walking again. I follow.

"Not literally," she says. "I mean, maybe. Who knows. I was meditating, for hours, a really intense session, and I got out, beyond the tunnel, but it wasn't the moon on the other side. It was a different kind of space. Pure white. It was trying to push me back. There was all this gravity and density. It felt like there was a rock forming in the back of my brain. Becoming heavier and heavier. Pressure started building. It felt like it was cracking my skull. I held my nerve for as long as I could, but it was like my brain was being pushed apart from the inside out. When I opened my eyes the pain evaporated, and there it was, on the ground in front of me, the exact same size as I'd felt it in my head."

"The stone?"

"Right in front of me."

"Where were you?"

"In the back garden."

"And it was just sitting there in front of you?"

I'm finding this story a bit of a stretch. My head is still partially in the restaurant with the smell of pizza bread and garlic, the soft complexity of low-volume Bach, Nino's heavy arm on my shoulder, a boring couple who may or may not be in love whose table needs clearing. Farzaneh notices my complacency, which is surprising.

"Look," she says, "I'm not sure what happened, or how it got here. But when I reached out and held it, I felt something. Something special. I don't know how to describe it. It was like a sensation of home, telling me that I'm ready, that I'm in the right place."

"Ready for what?"

"I can't explain it. It's not really tangible."

"You know, it was my last shift," I say, looking back down the road. "I didn't get to say goodbye."

"I thought you'd want to share it with me. I thought you'd want to know."

"I do. I do."

"Come on then."

"Where are we going?"

"To plant it."

"Plant it?" I turn my neck back towards the restaurant again. "I think I'm going to go back. Just for a minute."

Farzaneh carries on, away from the restaurant.

"I know you think I'm crazy but have you never seen something and just known that it was linked to your existence in some way. You were meant to have it, because it would help you get to where you needed to be?"

"The first time I saw you maybe."

She glances at me with dismissive joy.

"You're intuitive with people. I know you are. But this is different."

"I'm not sure it is."

"If it isn't, then you understand. Maybe that feeling you had was all part of it."

I recall the mesmerisation I felt in that moment when I first saw her, sitting on Shaun's bed. The black hunger in her eyes pulling me in from across the room, something eerie and intangible telling me that she was my future, she was the place where I belonged, where I always needed to be.

"I don't know about this," I say, nonetheless giving up on going back to Nino and the restaurant and committing to walking with Farzaneh.

"You're part of it," she says. "I don't know how yet, but you are."

She leads us down the road to Tower Hamlets Cemetery and along the path to the rainbow bench. I follow her past the white tombstone with the seven white moons and into the hidden enclave in the bushes. She claws into the ground, digging a small hole, then carefully places her moonstone in it. After covering it and patting down the soil she turns to me.

"Can you feel it?" she says. "This is the place."

I hunch my shoulders and attempt a look of facilitation. I feel alone, and like the world is too big and the skies are too high. My life has no direction, nothing is fixed. Farzaneh looks up at me as though she simply can't believe my ignorance, that it must be wilful. The significance of all of this is so present. The meaning is so close.

FOUR

Farzaneh is watching a row of white cherry blossoms rain their petals over the edge of a pasture from the train window. I'm sitting in the aisle seat, reading Spinoza's *Ethics*. I submitted my dissertation a couple of days ago and all of my university work is now officially finished. I should be facing the great problem of finding a place in the world, not indulging Farzaneh's spontaneous request to visit Stonehenge, but going to see an ancient monument seemed like a reasonable way of escaping the future for one more day.

"You know, there's an orchid that is always at its most fertile during the full moon," says Farzaneh.

There is a factual whimsy in her voice that seems uninterested in any potential response I might have. I look up from my book. She carries on looking out of the window.

"Oh?"

"It adapted to the moths that pollinate it."

"Interesting," I say, wondering if I'm going to be able to get back into my reading without engaging any further in this conversation.

"The moths came to them more when the moonlight was brighter, so they changed their nature."

Something about what she has said, the logic of it, has unsettled me. I imagine she's trying to link herself to these orchids, as though their fertilisation rhythms and her menstrual cycles are the same. They are part of a mythic nature, symbiotic with moon cycles, beyond the realm of ordinary plants and mortals. I feel impelled to shut the concept out so I cross my legs towards the aisle and go back to my reading.

We get off at Salisbury and catch the heritage bus to the Stonehenge car park. There's an entranceway where we pay, then a gift shop and a café, all dug into the ground so as to make as little visible impact on the site as possible. Emerging from this visitor's bunker, we approach a low-strung rope about thirty metres from the stones and a small sign telling us not to cross. Between thirty and forty people are scattered around a woodchip path that orbits the monument.

"They're always putting fences around things," says Farzaneh, annoyed by the restriction. "They can't imagine that it's the same world on either side."

"I suppose they just want to preserve it. Before it was like this, when you could just park up and wander over, people used to turn up with hammers and chisels and take pieces of it home with them."

We pause, taking in the construction. The vertical, stacked rocks are blazing in the sun, gleaming with implausibility. Farzaneh's face expresses an inert but satisfied appreciation, as though she is sharing a secret with the stones. Some silent string in me tugs and I'm moved into jealousy.

"Things can't change their own nature," I say, a vague thought from earlier coming into focus.

"Sorry?"

"The orchids. Surely it was just that the ones that were more fertile at that time of the month had a better chance of surviving and passing their qualities along."

Farzaneh's eyes shift into a bored sympathy, pitying my obvious logic.

"Nothing can accidentally align with the lunar cycle," she says, setting off, walking around the path. "Because it never quite takes the same amount of time. It takes determination to maintain that kind of change."

"You think these orchids are free to choose how and when they blossom? They've evolved some kind of will?"

"More and more I feel like there is a will in everything, underneath it all. If you focus on certain things you can let it in, let it change you."

"So, you think the universe has a plan now?"

"I'm not saying that anything is preconceived, just that chaos and collision don't account for everything. There's more to life than survival and mutation."

"But you are saying that the will of an organism can influence the material world."

"Think of it this way," she says. "The moon changes the amount of moisture in the air, by moving the tides, and moisture in the air changes the levels of moisture in plants, and when the moon is full there's a very particular level of moisture. Slowly, these orchids learnt to listen to this different stream of information inside themselves, separated it from rainfall, prioritised it over sunlight. They accessed a deeper understanding of their nature, and then they changed. It wasn't a conscious will in the way you or I think of consciousness, but the same abstract laws were applied."

After this explanation my flare up of anger and jealousy recede. I feel as though she has illuminated a tiny portion of her private world. I'm enthused by her openness and something about this orchid idea seems to chime with what I've been reading. Spinoza's is a world that learns from itself, where intelligence lies within the structures of everything, and life pushes itself towards a greater comprehension of itself.

"I've got to admit, I like the idea of a plant learning that the moon is just as important as the sun," I say, "and all because of moths that they can't see or hear or feel."

"Exactly."

"It is amazing, when you think about it."

We carry on walking, around the shady side of the stone

circle. Farzaneh takes lighter steps, happier and more open now that I have conceded to the reasoning behind her orchids' ability to connect with the moon.

"When I was younger," she says, "after Mum died, before Dad got cancer, when everything was happening with the moon, I bought into all the pagan stuff for a while. I even came here for the solstice a couple of times. I guess I was hoping for some kind of feeling of rebirth, or renewal. I can't remember who put it all in my head, I was hanging out with some weird people, but I started to believe in a primitive era when every woman menstruated in line with the lunar cycle. I decided that women were closer to nature than men. We were like those moon orchids, reading the natural flows inside of us, and men were just primates, barely able to listen to anything beyond their basic needs and egos. Of course, in this version of the world, I was the last of nature's women, the moon's only remaining wife, and all the modern people had lost their way."

"That sounds romantic," I say, confused because these were the assumptions I was making about how Farzaneh was thinking just two minutes ago.

"No," she says. "It was a fantasy. I was using my connection with the moon to separate myself from everything else. Divisions are just habits of thinking. Limits we draw for ourselves. Primitive and civilised, nature and culture, self and other. They're all just ropes we string around things, so we feel like we understand them, but really they leave us isolated, staring in from the outside, disconnected."

"But there are divisions in life. Differences. Limits."

"No. There are spectrums, and the truths beyond them as they blur into nothingness. I think I'm finally learning to see beyond them, to what underpins it all."

"You can't unsee reality."

"What if you can?"

"You can't."

"I thought the connection I had with the moon was in my

womb but I've stopped menstruating. And I still feel it. I'm starting to feel it in my bones. In my breath even."

My eyebrows furrow with worry.

"You're not eating enough," I say. "That's why your periods have stopped. You need to start looking after yourself."

"No," she says, turning her head away from me and back to the stones. "I'm getting close."

She takes a moment to breathe and then steps over the boundary rope and starts walking towards the monument. I feel torn from her, stuck behind the rules of the rope. I watch helplessly as she walks in and among the circle of rocks, running her fingertips along their surfaces, looking up and around. She stops by the broadest side of one of the slabs in the centre and rests her face on it. Her hands move out across the surface, arms opening, trying to release herself to an object that is too big to behold. I have the sensation that events on the other side of the rope have a connection with a world that I can't grasp. Farzaneh looks as though she has found a place that I could never take her to.

I look nervously from side to side but nobody seems to have noticed her breach, or they don't care. Then a barrel-chested man in a high-visibility security vest walks up from the visitor's bunker and says something into his radio. I'm immediately anxious about protecting Farzaneh so I step over the rope and start jogging towards her. A tall man in outdoor gear stops taking a picture of his family and stares at me. His two teenage daughters take out their mobile phones and start filming me. Now that I have crossed the divide, people are becoming excited and interested. I can feel their eyes and the intensity of their attention on me, and I feel self-conscious about my movements as their recording devices capture my actions.

The security man, startled by my dash towards the stones, steps over the rope and rushes towards me with his spine and stomach bent forward. I speed up, ending up in among the rocks by Farzaneh's side. The security man reaches the outer circle flushed and panting. He slows to a stop and takes a moment to appraise the situation. Farzaneh looks to have melded with her rock and is oblivious to my presence. I turn back towards the security man. After holding eye contact with me for a moment, he decides to persist and, frowning, moves in closer with his hand on his holstered radio as though it is a gun that he is nervous about using.

"Please," I say, holding my palm up towards him. "Just a minute."

He is hesitant and defensive about my stance so I soften my posture and try to make the halting gesture more of a peace-keeping request. He looks relieved that I am coherent and passive and that he might not have to deal with me in an aggressive manner so he nods, grudgingly, to let me know there is very little leeway with this minute that I've requested and that it ought not to be a minute at all.

"You can't be here," he cautions.

"No. I know."

He looks around at the people staring over at us.

"One minute," I say. "Please."

He nods again and stands by the outer circle. I step to Farzaneh's side.

"Far, we have to go."

She turns her face towards me and opens her eyes with a smile.

"I can feel it," she says. "Through the surface. I knew I'd be able to feel it."

There is belief and amazement in her expression. I'm standing in a different universe to her, one of stacked rocks and open plains, of cars on a nearby road, of people on the other side of a low hanging rope.

"We have to go back."

"It's everywhere," she says. "In every tiny piece of everything."

"We can talk about it on the train. Right now, we have to leave."

"Feel," she says, gesturing for me to put my hand on the rock, her body still flat against it.

I place my hand on the surface of the vertical stone.

"Do you feel it?" she asks.

"No," I admit.

"You have to learn how to surrender."

"Come on, let's go. You're going to get us locked up."

She looks around, wary of those who might take away her freedom, and withdraws her body from the rock.

"It's in the stone," she says, smiling. "It's everywhere. I know why they built it."

"Come on. Let's get going."

"It's a map. It shows you how to find it."

I lead her towards the part of the path nearest the exit, nodding my thanks at the security guard as we pass him. He glares at me, wary and suspicious. As we step back over the rope, the man and his teenage daughters stop staring and put their phones away. The slope in the angle of their shoulders conveys their disappointment at the lack of incident and, as we walk towards the exit, the intensity of being in their limelight simmers away.

FIVE

I skate towards the Thames. Twenty-one years old. A graduate. Two thousand years' worth of rational thought in my head. No particular future. The city surfaces are in constant flux. I navigate the angles, drops and rises. Skateboarding is more natural to me than walking. I ride as close to the river as I can. There are closed circuit television cameras everywhere. A bored security man walks to the front of his lobby hoping that I'm about to take a wrong turn down the side of his building or invade his car park. I grind the step in front of him to rile him, rolling and slipping away before he's able to react to the transgression.

I kickflip the steps across the road from St Paul's Cathedral, cross Millennium Bridge, then follow the river west, slaloming tourists, passing the Tate Modern and the corporate coffee shops and restaurants. At the Southbank Centre, I ride down into the graffiti-covered undercroft, the so-called birthplace of British skateboarding. I've never skated here before but I've seen it in so many skateboarding videos that it seems familiar. There are a few flat banks, some ledges and blocks, and a set of seven steps. An accidental skatepark. A by-product of modernist design. My eyes imbibe its flow and momentum. There aren't many people skating. It's daytime on a Tuesday. Just a couple of professionals with a shoestring camera crew, some loitering teenagers – finished school for their exams – and a small posse of rough-looking truants and drop-outs learning their ollies and kickflips.

I roll in and switch crooked grind the block, then switch nollie flip down into the flat bank. One of the pros shouts, "Yeah." I look over and fakie backside flip into my regular stance, so he knows the tricks I just did were in switch, with my weak foot forward. He taps his friend on the shoulder, says something in his ear and points my way.

I pop up my skateboard and survey my surroundings. I feel like every hour I've spent learning and grinding out the skill on my skateboard has been building to a moment where I'm capable of a physical act of self-expression, this moment. In my head, I am the antithesis to Farzaneh's inexpression, a driving force. She is so still these days, inert, moving inwards, away from the world. Without sex, or contact of any kind, she has been reduced to something that I see. I wake with the image of her, meditating, cross-legged in her Venetian mask, floating through my mind. A signal that exists but is nowhere. A thing that can't be touched. I have been skating away from this vision, pushing myself outwards, through the physical, into the world.

I spring and jump forwards. My feet connect with my board and I land rolling fast. One quick push and I'm at optimal speed. I kickflip backside 5-0 the long ledge, shove-it out, land in a nose wheelie, then 360 shove-it to a standstill. A whooping cheer rises and blurs as I keep on riding. The tricks I start doing don't have names. I focus on pressure points, knowing every little spring of my board and how to manipulate its forces, pushing with my feet and ankles, launching into the air and manoeuvring it with my legs and hands.

I twist off inertia with my waist and torso, moving with soft swaying swings before snapping into spins, wrapping the board's motion into my own, then stealing that motion, spinning around my board while it stays still. There is a toing and froing between rise and fall, turn and pull. I can feel the lines of the world bending, forces retracting, gravity and mass colliding. The act seems vital. I'm fighting to exist, to be present, to pull myself up off the concrete and be me.

I finish with my board upside down, one foot above, one foot beneath, hovering on the tip of the tail. With a twist of my arms and shoulders and a whip of my legs, I start spinning, moving my eyes back around to the same spot on the wall, using the flick of my neck to add momentum to the spin. My body and limbs are tensed into the shape of a capital K. The graffiti on the sidewalls swirls and then stops, swirls and then stops. After twelve or thirteen spins, I slow, crouch down, pushing pressure into the board, and then spring up. The board flips and spins. My knees are up by my shoulders. At the peak of my jump, my feet reconnect with the board and my body straightens. I land on the balls of my feet, perfectly balanced on the truck bolts.

There is a moment, before I feel the T-shirt beneath my hoody clinging to my back with sweat, and before my muscles pulse with blood, where I am in an ecstatic state, in the invisible centre of multiple worlds, body and mind, self and other, balance and chaos, beginning and completion. I look up. A small crowd of tourists has gathered by the entrance. They are looking at me, waiting for my next move, a couple of them filming me on their phones. I'm the only skater on the floor. The others are edged over on the sidewalls, also watching me. A couple of them begin banging the noses and tails of their skateboards against the concrete, shouting inverted complements: "Sick." "Dank." The tourists begin clapping. I look around, unsure how to escape the attention.

A couple of the younger kids jump on their boards and back into the fray of the park's curves and forces. This dispels the moment. Movements are beginning again, time has shifted on. A guy from the camera crew with short peroxide hair is skating over to me. His face is gaunt and he has wiry, sinewy arms dangling out of a new, heavily logoed skateboarding t-shirt.

"Where have you been hiding?" he asks. "Those skills were viral."

"I tend to skate on my own," I say.

"It's difficult to learn moves like those in a vacuum."

"I used to watch all the classic American skate videos when I was a kid. Rodney Mullen. Ed Templeton."

"I'm Dax, with Boarderline. You heard of us?"

He offers me his hand in a plunging ghetto shake that joins at the thumb. I oblige his hip-hop introduction.

"Sure. I've heard of you."

"We really need a decent flatland guy. We'd love to have you on the team."

"What would that involve?"

"Small cash advance, free boards, trainers, hoodies, a video spot, profiles in scene mags and video blogs, teammates, tours, competitions, product design – if that's your thing – routes into film production, content creation, marketing, company management. You join, you find the shape that fits. Sound cool?"

"Could I pay my rent?"

"How much is your rent?"

"Seven fifty a month."

"Probably not, man. Not for the first couple of years at least. And even then…"

"So what's the point?"

"The point is, you never know. It's all about hitting that spotlight and pushing the products out. Attaching your vibe to things. Most guys couch-surf for the first couple of years. Until they've got a few sponsorship deals in place. It isn't the steadiest game, but it's the best one. You know? We take it day by day. Figure it out as we go."

"I've got a place with my girlfriend. I need an income."

"Take my card. We can start out by making a little YouTube

slot. See how people take to your style. If you've got a job, we can work around it. Whenever you're free."

I leave his card hovering in front of me.

"Sorry," I say. "I don't think it's something I can sell."

"I get it. Trust me. I respect it. You need to keep something for yourself. Right? But this is about showing the world that there's more to life than sitting around watching TV. Showing them you can do something with yourself, with your body."

"Create content instead of consume it?"

"It's more than that. You know it is."

I look around.

"Southbank used to be a dump," I say. "Those first scene videos. There are heroin addicts in the background. Homeless people. The graffitiing they filmed was criminal."

"I know."

"Now it's as corporate as it comes. Tourists watching you from a safe distance, drinking Starbucks. Everybody waiting in line for their grind."

"We saved it from destruction. You must have seen us in the press. This whole place could have *been* a Starbucks."

"I know. It's good that you held on to the spot. Really. But first the skaters turn up, then young guys start buying cheap flats, then young women, families, then the investors arrive. All of that ground is paved by skaters. And, when big business comes, it tries to get rid of you, and when it can't get rid of you, because you start making their businesses look bad, they brand you. You become their unique selling point."

"Yeah, man. But that's life. We held tight. We've got our legacy."

"It's impressive. It is. But, it's a safe space now, an attraction. It exists to add value. A loss for an aggregate gain. The unwritten deal is that you have to be here. Exhibit your freedom. Your youth. That's the rent you pay."

"We still run wild on the city. You've seen the videos."

"When I was in high school, the idea of going pro, getting

paid to grind benches and jump steps, I can't tell you how big that would have seemed, but now, after living in London…"

I pull my backpack off, unzip it and take out my old copy of *The Last Days of Socrates*. The cover is buckled at the corners and the spine is ready to crack. I think of Socrates refusing Crito's offer of escape, fearless of death, choosing an alliance with Athens over a corrupted version of freedom. At the start of our relationship, Farzaneh said that Socrates should have fled from prison and I agreed. We were both for freedom at all costs. We thought that we owed society nothing. Now, I'm beginning to see why Socrates had to stay, why he had to accept his social contract. I chose London and its rent. I chose education and its debt. If I want to be here, I have to pay my way. I offer Dax the book.

"You should read this."

"Yeah? What's it about?"

"Holiness. Arrogance. Saying things the world doesn't want to hear."

"Sounds intense."

"It is. Everyone should read it."

He takes the book, flips it over and back again.

"I will." He holds out his card. "Call me, man. I want to get those skills on camera."

I take his card: *Dax 'the Wax' Rimmer – Boarderline Skateboards. Communications and Marketing.*

"Thanks," I say, nodding, "I'll think about it."

I jump onto my skateboard and ride back into the city.

SIX

I walk into a recruitment agency in a pair of synthetic black trousers and a crinkled shirt. The woman at reception gives me a form to fill in. The chairs in the waiting area are too low. My knees rise above the table in front of me. All the plastic and polyester surfaces are grey and purple like the agency's logo. The main portion of the office is partitioned off but I can hear telephone calls being taken by faux-enthusiastic voices, making arrangements with new recruits and employers.

I'm sent into a room to do three computer tests: typing words and numbers, navigating a word document and navigating a spreadsheet. They are all skills that I've had since primary school. After getting a degree in Philosophy, spending three years thinking about ideas and how to structure arguments, the part of my brain that deals with these basic computer skills barely makes an impact on my stream of thought.

A woman in a shiny grey suit walks over to me looking down at a print out of my results. Her teeth are beginning to brown from coffee. She is morbid but denying herself the right to her own depression, squeezing out her last drops of positivity before her eyes cave in.

"Excellent. You got perfect scores."

"It was just basic stuff."

"You'd be surprised how many people can't do basic

stuff," she says, forcing a laugh. "We've got a position that we need to fill quite urgently and I think you'd be a good fit. Could you start tomorrow?"

"What is it?"

"It's in the financial services sector. You'll receive full on-the-job training and nine pounds an hour for the first twelve weeks. After your probationary period, they may or may not decide to take you on permanently. The starting salary, at that point, is eighteen thousand a year. Either way, you can come back to us here if you want something else. How does it sound?"

"Financial services?"

"A great opportunity for a graduate. And Canary Wharf is so close to you, over there in Hackney. What do you say?"

"Tomorrow?"

"That's right."

"And there's no interview or anything?"

"This is the interview."

"Sure. I'll give it a go."

"Great. I'll let them know you're coming. I'll email you the details and a timesheet this afternoon."

Sitting on the bus in office clothes, I feel like an insignificant decimal point in an economic superstructure. Money is everywhere, dragging people across the city like an invisible moon. Commuters crowd the pavements, moving in a dejected murmuration, somehow avoiding an endless chain of collisions. People on the bus stare down at their phones, thumbs scrolling through pictures of children, popstars and advertisements, some of them with ear buds in, slumping their heads, watching TV shows or video blogs. A small portion read the free newspapers full of media-focused current affairs. Others, wearing hip corporate headphones, listen to music, forging a soundtrack over their lives. The way to act seems to be about distraction, trying not to notice each other or the mutual loss of will and self-direction.

The on-the-job training is forty minutes with a preoccupied, mole-faced man who takes me through the in-house database and then leaves me with a small pile of standard operating procedure print-outs which give step-by-step instructions for each of my daily tasks. The job is exactly how I imagined all desk jobs would be. There is typing information into spreadsheets and databases, making various arrangements via email and telephone, digital record keeping, and a half hour lunch break. The work is constant, there is too much in fact, but computer programmes do most of the thinking.

There is a lot to take in on the first week; meeting new people, learning new computer programmes, contextualising the work and the nuances of its language, but as everything becomes known, and the monotony of all the future weeks begins to dawn on me, a dull anxiety creeps in. The first five days feel like they undo five years' worth of education. My brain is needed in a purely mechanical way. The people in the office seem to have found peace with this reduction by checking their phone messages, browsing websites or breaking off for coffee whenever they feel the itch to be more than someone who feeds a machine.

After twelve weeks and the offer of a permanent contract, I find myself obsessively deconstructing the death of Socrates over and over in my head: his loyalty to Athens, staying in prison with the option of escape, laying down his life for the city that stole his freedom. Unlike Socrates, who got to walk around and talk to people all day, develop his thoughts and ideas, and enter into discourse with the people in power, my allegiance to London means eight sedentary hours isolated in front of a computer screen, losing touch with my thoughts and ideas, and disappearing into a faceless system. It's difficult to know whether I'm thinking too highly of myself or if the principles of the social contract no longer apply. Surely, when society is governed by an ideological monopoly, it shifts the context of a citizen's loyalty and, by preventing alternative lifestyles, it also changes the meaning of freedom. I leave the employment contract open on my desk on the signature page for days. The empty dotted line gains a coffee ring. I put it away in my desk drawer.

In the evenings when I get home I'm too tired to skate or read. My body feels limp and my eyes are fuzzy and dry. Instead, I slump on the couch and stare at Farzaneh, meditating in the middle of the floor in her Venetian mask. She barely speaks or moves anymore and I've come to accept this. I begin to wonder if she is doing the right thing by opting out and watch her, between meditations, gnawing on a carrot stick or a sugar snap, the way a child watches a squirrel with a nut; initially excited by the potential of her wild nature but, ultimately, bored by her inane self-regard.

All the while, skateboarding tricks fade from my muscle memory and my poise in gravity loses the diamond point of its centre. The linguistic complexity of my thoughts begins to fade too, along with my ability to objectively interpret my environment. With these diminishing returns of self, my values and principles also begin to wither, and in my less esteemed state it dawns on me that the bottom line is that I'm no exception. London has no outside. You're either in it or you're not. And, one day, when Farzaneh's money runs out, she'll have to face this fact too. So, I sign the contract. I commit to the office job. What Socrates would or wouldn't do doesn't matter. I need to pay my way like everybody else.

I'm walking home, some time in some day, long enough after they've taken me on to feel like there was never anything else. My eyes are aching from being in front of the screen all week. It must be the weekend because the sun is high in the sky. Picking at a splinter in my finger, I turn down our road and straight into the path of an old woman carrying a cheap mass-produced lamp with a familiar-looking crease in the shade. I try to sidestep her but she meets my step. She has six white hairs sticking out of both of her cheeks and dark blue veins in the bags under her eyes. Something about not being able to get out of her way makes my stomach turn. I'm more anxious than I should be.

"Thank you," she says, smiling.

I don't understand why she's thanking me. It doesn't make sense. I grimace and sidestep her with a jagged lurch, feeling like something terrible is coming.

As I get closer to the house, two burly Russian guys walk past me carrying what looks like our couch. There's a young woman across the road struggling to keep our coffee table on her back. I twist my neck. I can't see her anymore but I'm suddenly sure that the lamp the old woman was carrying was ours too. Outside the house, two of our chairs have been left unguarded, waiting to be claimed. I walk down the steps and open the front door.

"Farzaneh?"

Everything looks the same in the hallway.

"Farzaneh?"

I put my coat on the hook and toss my keys onto the metal plate on the cabinet. Turning into the living room, I see that it is completely empty. Every object has gone. It's just Farzaneh, naked, sitting in the centre of the wooden floor wearing her Venetian mask.

"What's going on?"

She doesn't stir. I'm struggling to focus. The room looks flat. Farzaneh looks too thin. She's become so bony. The purple feathers around her white Venetian mask are blurred and glistening. I feel like I'm waking from a long sleep. I have been lost in the rhythms of the forty-hour week, ignoring Farzaneh's monotonous existence and our deadpan divorce from one another. Somehow, this dull but bizarre existence has become normal. I've accepted it because nothing feels right, and no other path seems possible.

"Farzaneh?"

I stand in front of her and crouch down. Through the eyeholes, I can see that her eyes are open, still, fixed on the middle distance. She doesn't seem to have noticed my presence.

"Where's our stuff gone?"

No part of her acknowledges my question.

"It's not even our stuff," I say. "It's our landlord's stuff. How are we going to explain this?"

Her eyes flicker. She takes a deep, lethargic breath and drifts back down into herself.

"Too many objects," she says.

I find the presence of her voice almost startling. When did I last hear her speak?

"I can't do this anymore. It's too much."

I turn towards the bedroom.

"Please," she says, removing the mask and putting it by her side. "I need you."

"Need me?" I say. "You won't even let me touch you."

"It's just for now."

"It's been months. I don't even know how long anymore. I mean, what is this?"

"Calm down," says Farzaneh, struggling to stand up, wobbling with weakness. "You're helping."

"I can't do it anymore. You don't see your friends. You hardly eat. Your periods have stopped. Some of the things that you're saying… You're not well."

"We're getting so close," she says. "It's almost time."

"Close to what? It seems to me as though the moon is just going round and round while you wither away to nothing. When is it going to be over? When is it going to be enough?"

"One more month," she says. "It will all be over soon."

"A month?"

"Twenty-nine and a half days."

"And then what?"

"Then it's over."

"Okay So, another month. Then what?"

"I'm going to need you to do something for me. It might seem a little bit extreme."

"What?"

"I need you to bury me."

"Bury you?"

She takes a deep breath and glances up, looking for words and guidance.

"It's the only way."

"The only way to what?"

"The hole will be shallow."

"Have you heard yourself?"

"I'll be able to breathe, through a pipe."

"A pipe?"

"Please," she says, bringing the fingertip of her forefinger in front of her mouth. "This is how I find the way."

"What you're saying makes no sense."

"I'm going to try to explain it, but it's difficult. You'll have to really try to hear me. Going out there, working all week, it's changing you. It's changing the way you think, the potential of what you can see. You have to listen."

"I'm listening. I am. I always listen to you. How do you think it came to this?"

"Picture your mind and body for me, absorbing signals, forming perceptions, locating you, giving you a centre, a version of reality to work with and survive in."

"Okay."

"But imagine that, maybe, that process is like a radio picking up a radio transmission and producing a sound. There are lots of popular transmissions but the actual number of potential signals is infinite, and they're all sitting on top of each other. All you're doing is receiving and refining particular portions of the signal and making the wider field of information less complicated."

"So, I'm a radio and my mind is a radio station in this scenario?"

"Please. The kinds of waves I'm talking about aren't just in brains. They're in plants and trees, air and space. They run through everything. Secretly. Underneath the physical world.

And if you try, if you really try, you can find them. If you learn how to forget your eyes and your ears and your brain, you can go further."

"You sound like you might be having a breakdown."

"You said you'd listen."

"Fine. Go on."

"I'm getting so close, but I'm surrounded by all these competing signals. I can never quite break through. I need to cut out the interference, get rid of all the little things around me. Underground, I think I'll be able to go deeper, connect with the bigger signal, find the wider truth."

"I'm not sure this makes sense to me anymore."

"It makes sense to me," she says, resting her hands in the bony centre of her chest. "And don't you think it's worth it, even if it isn't possible, or I might be crazy? Isn't it still worth trying to understand something greater than the self?"

"It sounds dangerous."

"Trust me," she says. "The moon is showing me how. After the fast, it will all be over."

"Fast? You never mentioned any fast. You hardly eat anything as it is."

"The fast is part of it."

"For how long?"

"Just a moon cycle."

"A *month*?"

"Twenty-nine and a half days."

"No. You have to eat."

"Only air and water."

"A month without food? It's not even possible."

"People fast for much longer. Three times as long."

"I've never heard of anybody fasting for a month."

"It's the only way. I have to be pure."

I pull my head back onto my neck. She sees my reluctance but decides to move forward as though I've accepted her request. A note of confirmation crosses her face. She sits back down and crosses her legs. I look around the empty room, imagining our landlord's furniture scattering itself across the city.

"I need you to bury me on the full moon," she says, "fourteen days and eighteen hours into my fast. To attune myself. And then again at the very end, during the new moon. That's when I'll be ready. That's when the signal will be easiest to find."

"Two burials?"

"Yes."

I look away. The bare magnolia walls are throbbing and bulging. I'm beginning to feel like I'm losing my normal rational faculties, that I'm slipping into a dreamscape where the irrational and the impossible reign.

"If you're not going to be able to do this you have to tell me," she says. "I'll have to make other arrangements."

"It just all sounds so twisted."

"I know this last year has been difficult for you. I know you've stopped believing. Maybe you never believed. But there were moments when it passed into you. Seconds when you saw it. I could feel it."

"Maybe."

"Please. I need you to see this through. I need you to help me."

I try to tell myself that being buried alive is similar to being locked in a sensory deprivation tank. It's just new-age therapy with Farzaneh's slant on it. This positive thinking is fuelled by an image, born on the day we took those magic mushrooms together: holding hands on her bed, a lake between our arms, moonlight on the ripples of the water, our two bodies forming a single world. It occasionally rises up in me during moments of my deepest doubts, nourishing and reframing our relationship, filling me with a sense of hope. Part memory, part future, part longing, it exists in a place we never were, and a place we can never get to. I can see the lie but I can't outwit it. It's the most meaningful thing inside of me. When it's there I have to abandon everything for the image, push through every obstacle, try and get us to this perfect place.

"I need to read up on fasting," I say. "If it's safe, I'll help you."

"I want you to understand, it's not about moving away from you. It's about removing barriers, joining up with things."

"But this fasting. You've already lost so much weight."

"It's a cleansing ritual."

"When does it start?"

"I stopped eating today."

"I need you to promise me, if I do this for you, you'll come back. You'll start eating properly. You'll let me touch you. We'll be together."

"Yes," she says. "I'll always be with you."

This is the first time Farzaneh has ever expressed anything about our relationship which reaches beyond the present moment, the first sentiment that has stretched into an abstract and timeless promise. Always together. The hairs on my arms are standing on end.

"Twenty-nine and a half days," I say, wondering if I'm really going to help her do this.

SEVEN

I wake up before dawn, birdsong triggering shadowy images in my mind: digging up Farzaneh in the garden, the full moon beaming down, her pupils flitting around beneath the plastic of the snorkel mask, mud falling from between her scrawny legs, hair falling away from her scalp as I try to wash it. The burial has crept into me, more than a memory, it has become a series of snapshots lurking beneath the surface, a constant slideshow on the back wall of my mind. The world in front of me is filtered through the traces that it has left behind. When my eyes are closed it's all that I see. I reach blindly to my side with a flinching movement. Farzaneh hasn't come to bed. She hasn't slept by my side since she started her fast.

I get up and tread quietly into the front room but she's not in her usual spot. The kitchen door is open. She's outside, meditating in her Venetian mask, sitting naked in the hole. I watch her from the doorway. The moon has slipped down below the rooftops but its silver light is still present in the air. The conifers hide in their own shadows, etching charcoal cut outs onto a tinfoil sky. The surrounding houses' windows are still dark.

There is something primordial about the way Farzaneh's skin is clinging to her bones. She is a creature, able to access ancient memories. In the same way that a salmon finds the river, or a bird finds an island in the ocean, she is finding a far-off place where a human promise belongs. I feel drawn to her. There is a dark gravity pulling me in. Reality seems weighted here in the garden, with her.

I shower and then walk to and fro in the kitchen, eating toast and sipping coffee. My work clothes feel ridiculous on my body, a costume for a financial ritual. Farzaneh's nakedness contains power. Her straight-spine and level head assume meaning. But, as the sun rises and the sky pales, the air around her becomes wispier and less certain. The garden is beginning to mist. Putting my cup and plate in the sink, she fades. Our worlds are separating. My mind is moving towards concrete and steel, buses and commuters, and she is moving away, into the ineffable haze of her own consciousness.

At the office, I switch my computer on and, as the hard drive whirs and spins, I feel the momentary relief of a shift into a logical system. Part of me has become reliant on the satisfaction of overperforming in an environment where efficiency is valued over thought. I am one of the top five administrators on a floor of one hundred and eighty. My CPMs (clicks per minute) are through the roof. I've won a bottle of Prosecco on three of the five months I've been here. I'm the best at processing information, at having no opinion, at switching off and being no one.

As my screen lights up, my neurones fire and trigger muscles down my arms and fingers. I log in, sending rapid-fire signals through the mouse and keyboard into the machine. My tiny actions generate signs and changes on the screen, received by my eyes, and then I send more information around between mine and the machine's memories. Programmes and databases load. Emails sit unopened in my inbox. My cursor hovers over a button on the database home screen, an arrow over a pair of binoculars, about to click and search for something, but I pause, inert. Usually, in this moment, fresh from waking, stimulated by caffeine, my shift into the flow of high-functioning non-being is immediate but today I can't seem to remember what I'm supposed to do. The images and boxes on the screen are nonsense. All I want to do is think about Farzaneh. Love her. Watch over her. Help her find her way back to me.

Filling my water bottle at the cooler, Huan and Preeti are waiting for the coffee urn to boil, talking about looking forward to the weekend and laughing at a video clip on one of their phones, passing it back and forth. They live for the city, it's nightlife and culture, and they like to flirt with each other without crossing any professional boundaries. I search their mannerisms: feigning self-possession and amusement when really their laughter is nervous and emotionally bereft. They are lost between youth and adulthood, hoping that life's secret answers will turn up soon or they will be magically transported back into their youth. It occurs to me that I'm not like these two. If I stay here the answers I'm looking for are never going to arrive.

Noticing me watching them, Preeti turns the screen of the phone towards me and reveals a short section of the video they're laughing at: a goat chasing an old man down a dusty road in a South American country. It's herding him, with cartoon *WHAM!* and *POW!* signs appearing as it intermittently headbutts his hips and hind. I nod, bunch up my right cheek in a half-smile and go back to my desk.

"Can you get the workload stats over to me by eleven?"

I'm staring at a half-written email in which I'm trying to explain the reason that one of our procedures is the way it is and that I can't change the way things are done. Actually, I could make an exception, reject the procedure and make this person's life easier, but that would be breaking the rules. I shouldn't even be writing this email to explain things. There's a template email with a table from the website stating the turnaround times that I'm supposed to send out. Instead, I'm attempting to explain why I can't do a small thing for another person, justifying the protocol and, ultimately, framing it as humane – because of the other people who were in the queue before them – but I've stopped mid-sentence, selected the content of the email and paused, wondering why I'm not deleting it, sending the template, doing my job.

"Sorry?"

I look up at my boss, who seems to be taking my distraction lightly.

"The workload stats, for OBS and the group inboxes."

"Sure," I say, deleting the body of my email and clicking into the template folder. "Right after this."

"Great."

She smiles a phoney smile that cracks her cheeks into shards. I wonder when she crossed the bridge into a world where a smile signifies that everything is running just how we've been told it should, that the stats will arrive on time and that this result is an approximation of joy. She hunches her shoulders a little, gives her smile an extra little push and then walks away.

After completing the stats, I have the sensation that I wasn't there when I did them, that the attachment I'm sending could be a spreadsheet full of random pulls from the database, absolute nonsense. I can't see the strands of meaning between the columns and the rows, the numbers and boxes. It's all shaded by Farzaneh, buried in a hole in the garden, sitting silently in dirty bath water, her mind exploring abstractions impossible for me to comprehend. I send the stats anyway. They are probably right.

The afternoon is even less focused, digesting a supermarket-bought falafel wrap, struggling to ignore my tiredness, staring at the screen, drinking a strong coffee that is making my heart pound and cheeks flush just so my mind can maintain enough concentration to enter the data from a profit and loss account. The small business loan I'm working on is for a company called Zen Quality Assurance Ltd and halfway into its liabilities section, before my computer programme can infer the exact appropriate amount of debt for this company to be in, my will to persist through the alienating boredom of my work, to ignore my need to be with Farzaneh, hits a critical point.

I somehow know that if I strike one more digit on the keyboard's number pad something holy and precious will be extinguished in me forever. It would be easy, as easy as every other digit I've struck today, and in the grand scheme of the cosmos relatively meaningless, but for me, for my future and my sense of self, it would be irredeemable. Trusting my gut, I get up out of my ergonomic chair, step away from my well-organised desk and leave the building without a word, breathing in the crisp autumn air and toxic city fumes as I pass out onto the street through the revolving glass door.

On the bus home, I worry about my sudden departure and wonder which version of reality is truly more pressing: the world of work, where I earn money and accept the unavoidable presence of society and its costs, or Farzaneh's world, where systems are rejected in favour of the exploration of self and being. I exist in both but not fully in either, and each pulls me away from the other. Travelling between them, gravity loosens and I'm just here, myself, deliberating. I have the sensation that this moment, now, between the two worlds, is vital, that I need to use it proactively to fully understand my needs, but I end up daydreaming and breezing through useless thoughts.

Back at the flat, Farzaneh is meditating in the empty living room in her Venetian mask. Her malnourished flesh, drawing closer to her skeleton, makes me fear that I have chosen a path of neurosis and starvation, that I should go back to work, that maybe they haven't noticed I've gone yet, but I also respect her effort to search for a deeper truth, a truer centre, and her strength for trying to tune in rather than tune out. While she has been drawing closer to her chosen reality, I've been wilfully ignoring the conditions that give rise to the dynamics of supply and demand, selling my time and my labour, underthinking what I want my world to be, because the system is too powerful to displace, and too all-encompassing to avoid. Yet, over a year into her path, Farzaneh has managed to keep her back turned to it all, spent the whole time looking for another way. I can't help but feel, having witnessed the depths of her conviction, that she would have always found a way to walk her own path; inheritance or not. I am beginning to realise that, to me, she is becoming as large a figure as Socrates. She is the rarest kind of truth seeker, one of only a handful of truly individuated human beings in history.

"Far... Far..."

Her eyes stir. Vibrations between her body and the air produce a shadowy electricity, her inner being somehow connected to the surrounding space. Her skin and bones, just being, but fiercely being, are in deep time, primeval consciousness, a state where everything is raw and true.

"Please," she whispers. "Don't call me that. I'm not that."

"What? Far? It's your name."

"Not since... he died."

She slowly lifts her hands and takes her mask from her face. There is a bony ridge around her eye sockets, crevices beneath her cheekbones, a railing affect around her jaw. She opens her eyes but doesn't seem to see anything.

"A name is a word," she says, the sentence coming from a deep, faraway place.

"Have I neglected you?" I ask. "Have I let you slip away?"

"No."

"I need to tell you something."

She sighs.

"Trying to resist language..."

"I've left my job. I want to stay here with you."

"Want nothing."

"Will you let me?"

"You must fast."

"I will. I want to feel what you feel."

"Struggling... to speak..."

Sadness begins to well up in me. When I first met Farzaneh, language had the power to take possession of her. Words produced seismic shifts in her physical being. Her spine and arms would swing to the rhythms of humour, snap at argument and injustice, twist and twirl in the cadence of empathy and understanding. I used to think of her as being connected to her truth, constantly expressing it with language. All of that has changed. Her mind and body have cut the strings that once tied her to words. She has left the nuances of talk behind. Conversation is a microcosmic nothing, an irrelevant noise. She is seeking a greater experience of being, a sensory field which has no need for semantics. Knowing this increases the pain of her absence. I mourn the lost routes that language gave us, the illusion of using words to find each other.

"I love you," I say, declaring it openly for the first time, hopelessly, desperately.

No expression stirs on her face. Her eyes maintain their distance.

"Resist... the body..." she says.

"Farzaneh, I love you."

She closes her eyes.

EIGHT

I'm sitting in the hole across from Farzaneh, both of us naked. The pockets above her collar bone are cavernous. Her knee caps are wider than her calves. I close my eyes and try to focus on breathing but my thoughts slip toward food. I imagine chewing and swallowing apples, bread, cucumber, cheese, my jaw clenched and temples pounding. I pretend I'm meditating but there is no depth to my mind. My only success is that I haven't eaten anything, and that reflects a lack of action, a negation, so it feels false.

It gets dark an hour or so after the increased traffic noise of the school run, somewhere in the dip before rush hour. In that lull the temperature drops a couple of degrees and my body starts shaking. My concentration slips from scant to scattered. I go to the toilet for what must be the fifth or sixth time today and refill my glass of water at the kitchen sink. The garden is too cold to return to undressed. I can't face it. I watch Farzaneh from the kitchen doorway, my teeth chattering and body trembling, wondering how she remains so still and collected.

After a warm bath I go to bed and can't sleep because of the all-over hunger. My heart kicks in my ribcage. I have tiny scratching pains in my legs, little glitches and twangs in my chest and gut. The night drags and the symptoms of fasting push me towards paranoia. I wake up from doze after doze, unsure of the time, the place, who I am. There is the feeling that I'm a piece of string pulled taut from both ends with a tiny knot in the middle. The knot is my stomach, but also a fist, a protest.

When I finally give up on sleeping and get out of bed, I don't feel weighted to the ground. I'm that same piece of string about to fall in a bundle on the floor. I shuffle through blurred objects and unsure spaces to the bathroom. My sinuses are blocked. My throat and lungs are oozing. I cough up mucus and spit it into the sink, keep hacking it up, foul breath filling the air before my face, phlegm breaking free at the back of my throat. When it clears into a dry, husking cough, I brush my teeth, glad of the intense minty flavour, trying to resist the urge to swallow the foam for its nourishment.

I make my way to the kitchen, my hands on the walls. Farzaneh is still sitting in the hole. I drink a glass of water and go out and sit across from her. The grass is a muddy blue colour. The air's chill bites and nips at my skin. Above us, the crescent moon is bent like a sickle, sharp and thin, harvesting the dark sky. It's hard to endure looking at Farzaneh's shrunken body. In the pre-dawn light, the tips of her fingers have a black tinge to them. Wiry ligaments pull tight between her jaw and collarbone as she breathes. I can see her scalp through her hair.

Without meals, the present moment is endless, without pause or respite. Waves of nausea crash through bouts of nervousness and create fears of aneurism and death. The constant hunger is uncompromising and difficult to temper. A short trip to the kitchen is all it would take to throw away all my efforts so I rise to my feet, march indoors and start slamming all the edible contents of the fridge and cupboards into a large black bin liner. It happens in a blur of scrunching plastic wrappers and thudding glass jars. When I dump the bag outside the front door the world seems full of the threat of others so I rush back to the hole and sit down with Farzaneh.

With the possibility of eating diminished, I finally find

myself able to focus on my breathing; the cold air pulling in through my nostrils, filling my lungs, expelled through my mouth. The exchange of gases and molecules begins to sound like soft ocean surf on a faraway shore. My breath is mixing with Farzaneh's. I can sense our exhalations rippling and merging between us, two tides meeting and retracting, endless waves slipping into and over each other. I can't be sure how long it goes on, this symbiosis, but it feels new. My attention slips in the falling temperature. My body begins to shake. I open my eyes. Farzaneh's meditation is still strong and unwavering. I stand up with cramps in my legs and struggle into the flat, giving up for the night.

In bed, after another warm bath, my heartbeat is violent again. There's a cold sweat on my back. I can't think in any meaningful capacity. I'm hungry and feel like an amalgam of obscure pains and needs. My guts are slowing to a halt. The presence of my other organs seems more pronounced. In a drowsy moment, I become aware of all the little ridges and separations of my insides, and the insides of my insides, but also the sensation of the whole of my organism, the oxygen in my lungs moving into my bloodstream, the blood pumping through my body and into my brain, the relationship between breath and thought, time and existence.

I give up on sleep again and go out and sit across from Farzaneh. I have achy knees and shiver from the cold but as the sun rises the symptoms of my hunger begin to dissipate. My mind is alert and, although my body feels weak, I am more confident about fasting. The fear and presence of death is receding. There's a niggling absence in my gut, like my stomach has been surgically removed, but the desperation for food has gone. I feel like I was addicted to it and, now that I've mostly got the cravings out of my system, my mind is free to explore and think for prolonged periods without interruption.

My inner world comes into focus. Ideas, images and dream thoughts flit through my mind. Refracted memories bound out of a well of swallowed perceptions. I try to dodge these broken visions, dive beneath them, breath them out, keep following the centre. I move inwards, past glints of meaning on hidden shapes, down, into an underworld where powerful forces circle and open up before me. I know why Farzaneh has to do this now. I know because I'm beginning to have to do it too.

The moon slips behind Earth's shadow and the temperature drops. My ankles and fingers are translucent, revealing the blue veins beneath the flesh, but I've stopped shaking and the cramps in my legs are beginning to fade. I go to the kitchen and drink a glass of water. It crashes down the front of my gullet and stomach, clear and pristine. The clock's signs and numbers don't seem to mean much. My body is more attuned to the fact that it will be another night and day before the moon will reach its most central, darkest point. There is a sense of how many heartbeats it will take, how much orbit and rotation, the volume of breath. It is unclear to me where this knowledge comes from. I walk out and sit back down in the hole.

My meditations have changed. Thought used to be located at the front of my brain but my mind seems to run through all of me now. My limbs, chest, hands, feet, parts I used to think of as obedient pieces in the blind puppetry of my body, are now united. I exist entire, and the world around me reflects a furtherance of that entirety. The relation between the space I occupy and the space around me, the point at which my being ends and otherness begins, is both clearer and less sure. My mind is part of my body, my body is part of existence and existence is part of my mind. I find myself sinking into hidden places, without location, where everything is the same. Matter, all matter, and all matter one.

Time passes through the night and the day complete unto itself but then something new arrives in my consciousness. A small white dot. Low down, in the distance, where the moon is in relation to the world. As the Earth turns, it rises and grows inside of me, pushing away the surrounding darkness, transmitting a throbbing sort of static noise, growing bigger and nearer, its light beginning to overwhelm everything, arcing around my being. Just as I'm about to submerge, become lost in its whiteness, fear wells up in me. I realise that I can't feel my body. I can't breathe.

A rush of adrenalin pumps me back into myself. I'm holding my throat, in the hole, air funnelling into my lungs fine as a needle. I gasp and heave and cough. My heart thumps. Farzaneh opens her eyes and looks at me, studies me, my panic, the proximity of that light in my darkness. She understands what I have seen. I catch the faint glimmer of a nod. This is it, she's confirming. It's time.

She unbends her legs, digs an elbow into the grass and attempts to get herself upright. I stand up too, pausing while blood rushes to my head and back out into my body, my balance teetering and top heavy. Farzaneh stumbles and falls from a crouched position down onto her hand but I know not to help her, not to touch her, and she persists, shifts her weight onto her feet and slowly straightens her spine. We face each other, standing naked in the hole. Her head looks disproportionately large on her scrawny neck. Her eyes stare through me. I close my eyelids for a moment and slip in and out of consciousness, feeling like I'm falling into her and out of her as I breathe, her skin and bones evaporating and re-forming.

Farzaneh carefully steps up out of the hole and onto the lawn. It is unclear whether her caution is a symptom of physical weakness or if the time around her is moving at a slower rate. Her next step takes five seconds to form in her mind but when it comes it has a lurching definition. The step after this comes quicker still. The pathways between her being and her actions are beginning to bridge. I look up at the black moonless sky while she regains the fluency of motion. When she makes it to the kitchen door, I grab the shovel and follow her in.

In the bedroom, Farzaneh's bony limbs begin slicing through space and time with efficiency and poise. She puts on a white cotton dress which hangs lank from her shoulders and then grabs some white pumps. I get dressed too, my jeans loose around the waist and buttocks and my hoody baggy beneath the armpits. I look in the mirror and notice that my face is less bloated with sugar and fat. My cheek- and jaw-bones are more defined and my gaze into myself is more intense and direct than it used to be. Farzaneh shoves the snorkel mask and the Venetian mask into my backpack behind me. I turn and she zips it up and passes it to me to carry.

On the street, Farzaneh walks ahead of me, sure on her feet now, moving with a catlike finesse. I struggle to keep up. The street light is blurring my vision. It's just her in the centre, moving away into wavy bars of urban amber. The spade clunks against a rivet in a garden wall beside me and almost trips me over. I spin on the balls of my feet, looking for a stranger who might expose us, ruin everything, but see nobody and rush to catch Farzaneh up.

Walking across London Fields, figures appear beneath the white beams on the paths and then slip back into the darkness beneath the large plane trees. As we cross a footpath, a cyclist with a blinding LED light speeds out of a shadowy nowhere and swerves around us. Fear swoops through me. For a moment, it is the light from earlier, the engulfing, arcing light, come to obliterate me. Farzaneh doesn't flinch. Her path forward is inevitable. There are no external threats. Just one future certainty.

Broadway Market's pubs and restaurants spill people out of their doorways, creating semi-conglomerated huddles of smokers and gabbling drunks. The crowd noises swell as we pass entranceways, which exhale warm, alcohol-soured air. I look down, avoiding eye contact, following the white heels of Farzaneh's pumps. I hear an obnoxious young woman say, "Oh my God". The voice shoots between us, and I know that she is referring to Farzaneh, her emaciated appearance, but I resist the urge to look up.

On the canal's towpath, passing by Globe Town, a small

gang of teenagers lurk beside a moped, smoking weed and drinking energy drinks. A couple of the boys are showing off to a girl, the rest are chatting sullenly and looking at their phones. A group of overweight girls cackle as they pass, talking disparagingly about the boys around the moped. Seemingly unable to see us, one of them knocks my shoulder and ignores the contact. I feel spun around and woozy, the knock seems seismic, like it might send me into the canal, but Farzaneh is off ahead again, veering out through Mile End Park. I have to keep up.

To get over the black iron gate at the cemetery we have to climb onto a yellow gravel bin and then higher onto a green electricity box. Although Farzaneh doesn't seem to have any muscles left in her body, she springs over the gate and lands with perfect grace and form. Dizzy from the exertion of mounting the electricity box, I pass her the shovel over and dangle and scale down the other side using some thin sycamore saplings to break my spinning fall. Pain fills the centre of my feet as I land, as though nails have been driven through them. I crouch in the shadows waiting for the feeling to subside.

Farzaneh shimmies out of her dress and pumps and walks naked out of the shrubs into the cemetery. I grab the shovel which she has left lying by her discarded dress and skip to catch her up, passing white crosses and Virgin Marys on the left and the stone wings of angels on the right. What I'm seeing and perceiving, the shapes and colours of the statues in the night, Farzaneh's bare back and shoulders at this exact angle, at this exact time, all seems chiselled into the moment, part of an orchestrated plan that I don't quite know all the details of. A a decapitated saint on the corner of the row confirms the inevitability of it all, and the need to submit to a higher form of logic. I am a mechanism in an unchangeable truth and must accept that I perceive it from the outside, with freedom and chaos swimming in the air and consciousness around me.

Carrying on down the graveyard's spine, Farzaneh stops

to look up at the dead space where the moon is lurking, invisible, dragging oceans around the planet, then she veers off the path, in among a cluster of slanted crimson cenotaphs, moving faster and more assured. I dash after her, my backpack rattling and arm crooked to keep the spade from catching against the ground and graves. My foot falls unexpectedly into a deep pocket of earth, jarring my knee, then a few strides later, still unsure, it lands on a raised stone border beneath the overgrown grass. My ankle turns and I fall to the ground. The blank eyes of a mournful male statue in long robes look down into mine. His stony grief, his sense of loss, and the note of worry he has, seem particularly well executed for a graveyard sculpture. He has a living empathy that produces a piercing sense of panic in me, an anxiety that I am desperate to ignore. I rush to my feet and continue after Farzaneh.

Emerging from a cluster of trees I see the rainbow bench and the sharp points of Farzaneh's shoulder blades moving in among the bushes on the other side of the path, slipping through the cracks in the ivy and thin branches. I run over and struggle to make my way through the knotted mass of foliage, tearing and stumbling into the enclave beyond.

As I step into the clearing, a firework bursts somewhere above us, followed by the distant whelps and squeals of excited teenagers. The light from the explosion slips through the cracks in the treetops and bathes us in an electric blue light. In the last instant of its luminescence a thousand living shadows rush from branch to branch in the trees and bushes and I lose sense of forward and backward, up and down.

Farzaneh reaches towards the ground, pawing at the earth and plucking out something small and white; the moonstone she buried. It glows in her palm, creating a dim moonlight in the enclave. I'm confused because it's barely the size of a pea. When she buried it, it was almost the size of a tennis ball. Its size and its roundness made it unusual. Yet, somehow, I know it's the same object, the same thing in a different form.

Compressed. Shrinking, even as she holds it. I can see the movement of its retraction on her palm.

Farzaneh tilts her face up towards the sky, watching, or listening, and puts her palm against her mouth, swallowing the small white stone. The underlying darkness thickens and, as it does, a soft white light begins to gleam around the bony crevices of her body, rising off her skin as though she is dusted with magnesium. I'm dumbstruck, staring at the glow. Farzaneh looks down at her shimmering skin, unmoved, simply raising her arms to confirm its presence, then she grabs the shovel from me and starts digging, driving the head into the ground, churning through tough, cold soil like earth is air and air is earth.

When she is standing in a hole the same size and depth as the one in our back garden, glowing white in the dark, she sits down and starts to meditate. The enclave, the night, the bushes and the trees, they all breathe with her. Space and time stretch and bend with the movements of her lungs. I can feel the fabric of reality warping through me. I take the mask from the backpack and put it down beside her. Without opening her eyes, she reaches out, puts it on and lies down. She's ready.

Even I can feel the new moon approaching now. I am attuned to it somehow, reading it in the lightness and dryness of the air. There isn't much time. The shovel is waiting for me, leaning on top of the pile of mud, so I grab it and scoop up a spade full of earth. There is no weight to it. Gravity in the enclave feels loose and undone. I toss it over Farzaneh's glowing white form and she arches her back, pushing up into the cold sensation, a patch of black mud scattered over her torso, eager for more. I plunge the shovel back into the mound of earth and carry on, covering her spade by spade, limb by limb, until her moonglow is gone and she is beneath the ground.

When I sit down beside the broken earth and close my eyes, I have the sensation that I'm falling, slipping away. The walls and lines between objects and spaces disperse. I begin to feel Farzaneh's presence around me, beyond me, in a deeper space, but the more I try to find her, connect with her, the less distinct she becomes. Focussing on her location only gives me a relative position, placing me. I don't have the same capacities that she does. The pathways out towards her collapse and fold. Our divisions re-form. I'm just me, embodied, alone in my mind.

Dry leaves crackle and shiver in the autumn breeze. I look up through the trees. Two hundred and thirty-nine thousand miles away, the moon is slipping into the centre of the Earth's shadow. This is it, the defining moment of Farzaneh's ritual. All of the fasting and searching and meditating has been in preparation for this moment, when she can attune herself with the moon completely.

I hold my breath, trying to create as little disturbance in my being as possible. The moment of totality occurs, and passes, and the air around me falls empty. I exhale, confused and unmoved. The sense of predestination has fallen away. I feel lost, free, undone. And something is wrong. I've made a terrible mistake. My mind scurries into corners and recesses until the thought finds me: I don't know which mask I buried her in.

I lurch over and lunge into the cold mud, clawing at the ground, flinging handfuls of earth behind me. Within seconds a white slice of porcelain cuts out through the dirt and I stop, wrists trembling, jaw fallen. It's the Venetian mask. There was no air pipe. I buried her and she couldn't breathe. I quickly and carefully brush the dirt from the rest of the mask. The empty eyes stare up at me. I lift the mask from the soil, dreading the sight of Farzaneh's cold lifeless face beneath, but I can't see anything, only darkness. I stare down into the black fuzz, lowering my face.

"Far?"

I brush the mud gently with the side of my finger but it reveals nothing. I don't feel her skin, only dirt. Her face isn't there. The vague shape of a face is being brushed away by my finger. I clutch at a handful of soil, still nothing. I claw into the space where her neck should be, her ribcage, her heart and lungs, but it's all just earth.

I dig deeper and deeper into the ground, knowing that I'm too far down and that it doesn't make sense, pulling and tearing at thin fibrous roots, twisting and ripping at them until I'm scraping down into dense silt and clay, scratching at a thick, woody root, a foot further down than I buried her. The ground stops shifting and giving. The fingernail on my left forefinger rips off and the snap of pain stops my frantic scramble. My spine sags and my shoulders droop. I put my hands and face down into the bed of the grave and release a guttural despairing groan, losing myself, rolling round and round, trying to cover my body with any speck of earth that has touched her, twisting and turning, drilling my face and chest into the hole.

I end up on my back, looking up through the trees at the moonless sky, naked somehow, wearing the Venetian mask. Dead leaves fall from branches, alone briefly in their descent. A jet engine roars out a straight line. The sound of a siren fades as it moves towards somebody else's emergency. The city is carrying on. There is an emptiness in my stomach, a deep and desperate hunger. The darkness around me is too thick for a moth to find an orchid, and Farzaneh is gone.

Did you enjoy reading *Farzaneh and the Moon*? If you want to read more from Matt Wilven, here's an excerpt from his 2016 debut novel, *The Blackbird Singularity*.

ONE

An event horizon is a mathematically defined boundary around a black hole. It is the point from which light can no longer escape the pull of the centre and all possible paths lead further into the hole. Beyond it, gravity is thought to be so powerful that it stretches and tears matter into subatomic strings. Outside, observers see it as a black surface upon which things darken and disappear. They can use the boundary to calculate a few simple facts – such as mass, spin and charge – but they can only theorise about what happens in the space beyond it.

Lyd leaves the house for work around 7:30am. I'd been listening for the sound of her shower to stop but drifted off. I sit up and rub my face, annoyed about missing her. Lithium doesn't discriminate between the important and unimportant moments in life. My mornings are always fuzzy.

After using the toilet I look at myself in the bathroom mirror. The tired man behind the glass has aged a lot in the last two years. His black hair is mottled grey at the temples. The skin around his eyes is dark, bruised almost, but not on the surface; the beating has come from the inside. There is a discrepancy between the perceived morbidity of his character (someone in his late fifties) and the age of his physical body (somewhere in its mid-thirties) but his end is definitely closer than his beginning.

Downstairs, I make myself a coffee and a couple of slices of toast and listen to a John Lee Hooker compilation. The phone starts ringing after my first bite. I leave the music on and continue eating, letting it ring out. Lyd's left half an old packet of sultanas on the kitchen counter with a yellow Post-It note stuck to the front. It reads: *For the birds*. It's impossible to fault her pragmatism, thinking about feeding the neighbourhood birds minutes after seeing me sleeping through one of the definitive moments in our relationship.

I open the pack and smell them. They look sticky and are beginning to ferment so I open the sliding door and dump them on the frosty lawn. The majority fall out in one big clump and break into three pieces when they hit the hard earth. It's too cold to bother scattering them properly.

I slide the patio door shut, pull a chair away from the kitchen table, wrap my hands around my cup of coffee and watch the white lawn. Within seconds a blackbird arrives, and then another. Soon there are nearly a dozen of them fluttering about, raising tiny clouds of hoar frost and trying to win a few moments on top of one of the sultana clumps. I'm not sure how long I sit watching them but, for the first time in a long time, I experience the creative glimmer of a new idea.

After a couple of minutes the idea is outshining my interest in the birds so I venture upstairs to my writing desk. Words flow out of me all morning. There's no double-checking my email, no scrolling through news sites or vacantly gazing at lists of jobs. I don't even turn my computer on. I just sit down and write in my notebook for four hours.

Around lunchtime the broken images of the story stop appearing in my head and the words clog up. I realise that I've forgotten to take my lithium. I consider taking it now but what I just wrote felt like a breakthrough. I want to keep hold of this clarity of mind. I bite the inside of my right cheek and decide not to take it. I go out for a twenty-minute jog instead.

After a shower and some lunch I head back to my writing room. I stop at Charlie's bedroom door. It's been over six months since I've faced it, and Lyd doesn't like it when I go in, but I feel like I have to. My hand trembles as I reach for the knob. I wonder if I'm already withdrawing from my medication or if I'm genuinely afraid.

The room is exactly the same – off-white wallpaper with pleasant childhood objects dispersed like polka dots, planetary-themed carpet, *Toy Story* bedcovers, wardrobe cluttered with cartoon stickers and scribbled crayon drawings, plastic whiteboard with a picture of our family drawn in stick man form, a cheap wooden trunk too small for all the toys – typical stuff for a four-year-old raised in a London suburb. The only unique thing is the low-hanging moon I made for him in one of our make-believe sessions. I push it with the tip of my toe and watch it sway back and forth.

His favourite soft toy lies by the pillow on the bed. He was probably the last person to touch it so I don't want to disturb its position. It always looked like a limp, dead ferret, even when it was new, and we could never get it away from him. Where did it even come from? I look around and find myself sighing. The sound that comes out contains an unintended groan.

I pick up a retro 1960s robot from the windowsill; a toy we bought as an ornament. It's red, quite heavy and shaped like a squat cone. Its mouth is a chrome grill and the eyes are blue sirens. There is nostalgia in its naïvety, cuteness based on the fact that the original creator had been unable to form a clearer vision of the technological future. My jittery hands fumble and drop it.

The robot is motionless on the floor, part of the wrong future. I scowl at it, hate it, and find myself stamping on it three times. It doesn't break. It's surprisingly sturdy. The pounding hurts my foot through my shoe. Grimly amused by my failure to destroy it, I pick it up and put it back in the same position on the windowsill. My hands are steady again.

I begin to feel like I'm loitering so I leave the room and go back to my writing. I find myself working on another new story. It's set in a completely different time and place but it belongs in the same universe as the one I was writing this morning. I don't know how or why I know this. I just know that I feel alive in a way that seems forgotten. I'm focused and productive. Time is moving so fast that I almost can't believe it when I hear Lyd's key in the front door.

When people ask Lyd what she does for a living she usually answers with something self-deprecating like, "Sums." Sometimes, when pushed, she says, "I'm a physicist." Until four years ago she was an unsung hero in the world of particle physics and a some-time lecturer at Imperial College London. Then her book *Mini-Novas: The End of Science or the End of the World?* became a crossover hit (her publishers forced the subtitle – it upset Lyd for weeks but also ensured that she sold a lot of books). It's about the role of particle accelerators in the future of science and, specifically, the potentiality of mini black holes. Now she occasionally does interviews on the news when they need someone to balance out a regressive or scaremongering perspective. She used to work much longer hours but a mixture of success and grief has put her in a position to choose her own working pattern.

I rush downstairs to meet her at the door. She looks tired but her mood lifts slightly when she sees that I'm smiling. I pick her up off the ground with a hug. Outside's chill covers her.

"Wait," she protests. "Let me get my coat off."

I put her down.

"Hello, lovely."

"Hello?" she says, curious. "What's up? You seem pretty buzzed."

"It's just good to see you."

"*Okay.*"

"I'm sorry I fell back to sleep this morning."

"It's fine," she says, hanging up her coat and grabbing her leather satchel back up off the floor. "What've you been up to?"

She walks through to the kitchen, dumping her things on the counter.

"Writing. A new thing. A couple of new things actually. They might be part of the same thing. I don't know yet."

"Oh? That's good."

"The first taste is always the sweetest."

"Great. Angela's going to be happy."

(Angela's my agent.)

She kisses me, a peck.

"How was your day?" I ask.

"Dull. Busy. Mostly dull. I think the problem I'm working on might be impossible. And pointless. Impossibly pointless."

"In the simplest terms?"

"Diffeomorphism covariance."

"Should I pretend to—"

"No. It's fine."

"Prawn stir-fry sound good?"

"Later." She pulls an opened bottle of white wine from the fridge. "I've got a headache."

I accidentally lower the right side of my mouth as she pours out a glass.

"What?" she asks. "One won't hurt."

"No. One's fine."

I can tell from her slightly aggressive manner that she doesn't want to talk so I go back up to my writing room for an hour. After a quiet dinner we watch a couple of episodes of a political drama that we've been hooked on for the last few weeks. I can't follow the story because our silence feels like the most prominent thing in the room. I rest my hand on her thigh. I kiss the side of her face. She doesn't turn to me once.

Around 10pm we go up to read in bed but I can't focus on my book either. I pretend to leaf through the pages for a few minutes and then put my bookmark back where it was when I started. Once she's finished her chapter she turns her bedside light off and lies with her back to me. I turn my light off and nestle up behind her. When I put my arm over her she rests her hand in mine but doesn't say a word.

If you enjoyed what you read, don't keep it a secret.

Review the book online and tell anyone who will listen.

Thanks for your support spreading the word about Legend Press!

Follow us on Twitter
@legend_press

Follow us on Instagram
@legendpress